Past Poets
- Future Voices

2010 Poetry Competition for 11-18 year-olds

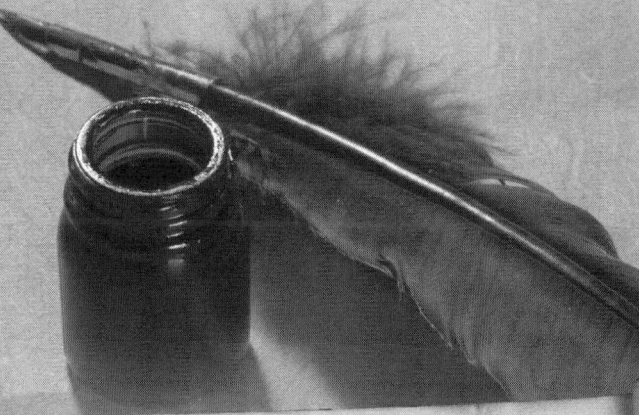

The British Isles

Edited by Vivien Linton & Lisa Adlam

First published in Great Britain in 2010 by

 Young**Writers**

Remus House
Coltsfoot Drive
Peterborough
PE2 9JX
Telephone: 01733 890066
Website: www.youngwriters.co.uk

Foreword

Young Writers was established in order to promote creativity and a love of reading and writing in children and young adults. We believe that by offering them a chance to see their own work in print, their confidence will grow and they will be encouraged to become the poets of tomorrow.

Our latest competition 'Past Poets - Future Voices' was specifically designed as a showcase for secondary school pupils, giving them a platform with which to express their ideas, aspirations and passions. In order to expand their skills, entrants were encouraged to use different forms, styles and techniques.

Selecting the poems for publication was a difficult yet rewarding task and we are proud to present the resulting anthology. We hope you agree that this collection is an excellent insight into the voices of the future.

Contents

The Elton High School, Bury

Thornaby Community School, Stockton-on-Tees

Ysgol Dyffryn Nantlle, Penygroes

Ysgol Eifionydd, Porthmadog

Ysgol John Bright, Llandudno

The Poems

Our New World

('Our new world' represents if we stop global warming)

The blazing sun becomes a light,
The Amazon a river
A spot among the frozen world
The Earth begins to shiver.

An animal runs the miles
Across the golden sands
The rivers sway from side to side
As the pattern flows to land.

Known creatures run away
Stars begin to form
Then we see the light of day
Because it is now morn.

Animals reappear
New crops are growing
Rivers run into the seas
And all our waters flowing.

Our new world is here now
Peace, luck and love
Our old world has disappeared now
So now there's flying doves!

Amber Brown (12)
Amble Middle School, Morpeth

1

Hidden Pain

Sun rose and then the sun set,
I'm alive but I'm dying every now and then,
I'm so upset.

So many tears were hidden behind each smile,
Each joy was giving sign that sadness is coming
in a little while.

Air became thunder,
Goodness became insolent but why, I wonder.

When love became the reason of agony then all the hopes
went to sleep,
I became victim of a painful arrow, I have a delicate heart,
and the wound is very deep.

I was running away from woes,
All happiness went away from me.
I'm tied up with grief chains,
I want to be free.

Black clouds have appeared on the blue sky.
I can't do anything else, I can just cry.

That is the pain of mine,
But still I tell others that I'm fine.

Sun rose and then the sun set,
I'm alive but I'm dying every now and then,
I'm so upset.

Shazia Latif (12)
Batley Girls' High School, Batley

2

The Aliens

The aliens are coming soon,
I saw them with the telescope on the moon.

They had no legs, no arms, no ears,
But had some eyes filled with tears.

Slowly, slowly they landed
And said, 'Happiness and love, that's what we want,

We didn't come to argue with you,
We came to share our feelings with you.'

But still the humans screamed and fought,
The aliens had no choice,
Heartless humans, is what they thought.

So after some while the aliens died and fell,
All the people said, 'What the hell!'

Nafisa Rahman (13)
Batley Girls' High School, Batley

Man And Sun/Son

There was a man
in the sun
he schemed and
shouted at his son

There was a man
in the sun
he schemed and
shouted at his son
He never knew that one day
his son would run away.

He schemed and
shouted no more
at his son
no more.

Colin Marshall (14)
Bearsden Academy, Glasgow

3

Teachers

I have loads of teachers
some skinny, some round -
some you would think weighed
about two hundred pounds

Mostly shouty and moany
but deep down I know
Mr Wards wants a pony

Miss Butlin is as small as her poodle
which thinks it is a bear
She takes that dog everywhere

But who I love the most is
Mr Torgeous, he is so gorgeous
With his big blue eyes
which are the colour of the ocean
you would think with all the time I look at him
I've been drugged by love potion

My teachers aren't that mean
I actually feel sorry for them
having to put up with many a teen
But all I'm sayin' is
when school's out for the summer
I'm defo drivin' home in a Hummer.

Hayley Hughes (13)
Bearsden Academy, Glasgow

4

Walter Smith

W alter Smith
A hero
L oves his fans
T ogether he thinks we can do
E verything
R angers lift another cup thanks to him.

S PL here we go - three in a row
M ighty manager
I rreplaceable in Scotland
(T ony Mowbry didn't stand a chance)
H eaven sent him.

Aidan McLaughlin (13)
Bearsden Academy, Glasgow

Rainbow

Red is like roses in the daylight.
Orange is like a beautiful day.
Yellow is like a sunny day that we can go to the beach.
Green is like long grass that I can lie on.
Blue is like the blue people in 'Avatar'.
Indigo is like the deep ocean.
Violet is like violet flowers.
The rainbow has lots of colours, including colours
that we don't even know.

Natasha McCarten (12)
Beechlawn Special School, Hillsborough

Rainbow

Red is like roses
Orange is like juice
Yellow is like the sun
Green is like grapes
Blue is like bluebells
Indigo is like my jeggings
Violet is like flowers.

Charlotte Keenan (12)
Beechlawn Special School, Hillsborough

Jewels Of The Rainbow

As red as rubies,
As orange as amber,
As yellow as a yellow diamond,
As green as emeralds,
As blue as sapphires,
As indigo as tanzanite crystals,
As violet as amethysts.

Harry Rouchy (12)
Beechlawn Special School, Hillsborough

Rainbow Spectrum

Red reminds me of blood and amputated limbs.
Orange reminds me of taco shells.
Yellow reminds me of bell peppers.
Green reminds me of gherkins.
Blue is like blueberries.
Indigo is like a stormy sky.
Violet is a very calm colour.

Francis Burns (12)
Beechlawn Special School, Hillsborough

Sad But True

God saw you were getting tired
A cure was not meant to be
So he put his arms around you
And whispered, 'Come with me.'
With broken hearts we loved you
As we had heard you had passed away
Although we loved you deeply
We could not make you stay
Your golden heart stopped beating
Hard-working hands at rest
God broke our hearts to prove to us
He only takes the best.

Kieran Boyle (14)
Bruntcliffe High School, Morley

Looking Down

Her face beaming
This bundle of joy
Through all the screaming
This little boy

His arms reached out
She held him dear
But she had doubt
An on-going fear

His eyes of almond shape
The large space between his toes
The imperfection and no escape -
She inevitably knows

His heart so big, so full of love
This boy's a gift, sent from above.

Sarah Forno (17)
Buckhaven High School, Buckhaven

7

Zero Hour

Cold, scarred soldiers stagger and fall with dread
Through thunder a barrage of bombs, whizz- bang
Across no-man's-land screams screech filled with lead
Young Germans scabbed with plague on barbed wire hang

Zero Hour. A horrified silence among the men
An awful ordure stench along the trough
Around soldiers clamber, whistles shriek then
Wav'ring falt'ring allies consumed by gas cough

Greeted with salvo, bodies tear and gash
Rapid machine guns spray all comrades brown
Thud, thud I fall to my knees, smell of ash
Ting, one final bullet. Dent in my crown

Motionless I lie surrounded by blood
Boots on my back buried in deep Somme mud.

Russell Grierson (17)
Buckhaven High School, Buckhaven

Memory Of Passchendaele

A thousand guns begin a symphony,
One by one we are sent to the abyss,
Writhing in pain, torture and agony,
A deeper and ever deeper darkness.

Whistling echoes, a moment of dread,
Rapturous blast throws bodies to the floor,
Young soldiers now buried where they once bled,
Beg it to stop, long to see this no more.

When will I wake, and the nightmare end?
Remember where forgotten souls lie,
Forget the shivers that their voices send,
In the trenches with their diseases, die.

Now at a standstill, nothing more to give,
Horrors of Hell I will always relive.

Ross Inglis (17)
Buckhaven High School, Buckhaven

Rainbow In An Oil Spill

Grim tormentor of nature's ache;
In the blissful sea of spillage of oil,
In creation 'tis the heinous snake,
A seabird absorbed by bleak yellow coils.
Man's benighted pollution casts her down,
Beauty burrowed beneath a baleful muck,
Impairing her flight, commencing her drown,
The glutinous corruptions have her struck.

When the giver of life doth smile below
Upon her helpless plight solution found,
A vision of reds, blues, pinks and yellow;
This melting pot of colours does astound.
No glimmer of hope had she glimpsed until
Beholding the rainbow in the oil spill.

Gemma Hastie (18)
Buckhaven High School, Buckhaven

The Game Of Life

'Honey, I'm home,' Ken came home with a smile
Cindy's friends were round; he knew just what to say
But she knew they would all leave in a while
And then the real Ken would come out to play.
Although her painted, happy face, she knew
He did not like to see her having fun.
The next day her face would be black and blue
It's not the end, the game has just begun.

'I slipped and fell, silly me,' she would say
When she was asked what happened, but her life
Was a game that she did not want to play.
This marriage roulette called being a wife.
Mum watched Jill playing over her shoulder
Praying life's different when she gets older.

Stephanie Kirk (17)
Buckhaven High School, Buckhaven

9

My Best Friend

I had a puppy
Spot was his name
He had nine brothers and sisters
They all looked the same

Lush black spots
With big blue eyes
He was so lovely
But that wasn't a surprise

From the first day I bought him
I knew he was mine
He was my best friend
I know he is mine

I came home from school
Early one day
Mum whispered the words
I saw him lay

Things were so bad
I turned really lame
He was my life
I just wasn't the same

Later that night
My mum said, 'Are you alright?'
I said, 'He was my best friend.'
She said, 'You will see the light.'

One day later

So . . . I went to see if my best friend was alright
And I saw a glimmer of hope
I realised it was his soul ascending to Heaven
Then I knew both of us were alright.

Kelsey Garbutt (12)
Carmel RC College, Darlington

10

Goldilocks - A Crook's Tale!

Once there was a girl with golden hair,
Who decided to walk into the home of a bear.
She could not stop herself from trying a chair,
That belonged to one of the bears.

Three chairs sat, carefully set,
Waiting for the girl to try their comfort,
One was too big, second as well,
But the third suited her rather too well.
As you all know, she broke baby bear's chair,
And I think that is totally unfair.
No chair would sit the woods surroundings
Oh my God, how outstanding.
If you're not yet persuaded,
Read on and see what else this naughty girl raided.

Next she went to get some soup,
But if you read on you'll see a twist in the coup.
Bowls sat fresh from the pot,
As you know two were hot and one was not.

Need I go on with this wicked little tale,
It should have never been put on sale.
It's obvious to me,
Why young parents can't see
That this little book
Is written about a crook!
Miss Goldilocks will be gone,
Punished for her sly behaviour,
So as for Goldilocks, she is now a failure!

Caitlin Heseltine & Holly Ferguson (12)
Carmel RC College, Darlington

Control Over Me

There was a time when you were all I could think about,
when I'd do anything for you.
Even though it's been a year now,
I wish you still felt that way too.

There was a promise of forever
and I'm still waiting for you here.
I should have known it to be untrue,
but still I shed a tear.

You hold my heart in your hand,
grasping onto it so tight.
I'd give up anything for you,
you'd be able to have me without a fight.

It's been so long since me and you
and other people have come and gone,
Yet my heart still bleeds for you,
telling me with you I belong.

I hate how you have the power,
the ability to control me.
Maybe if only one day
I'll finally be able to set myself free.

Free from your grasp,
my mind free from the thought of you.
My heart free and wanting for you to say,
'I love you too!'

Reanna Gamble (15)
Carmel RC College, Darlington

The Priest

A citadel of invocations.
A castle of secrets and fantasies.
A beacon of light for all those who are mislaid in being and spirit.
An enforcer of good and the chosen diety.

Sean Furphy (13)
Carmel RC College, Darlington

12

The Three Words

What a beautiful day
It'd been the best
Fun, games and music
With my friends and the rest

Stepped off the bus
Ran to my dad
Couldn't wait to tell him
What a great day I'd had

Before I could speak
Mum gently smiled
Took me by the hand
Talked to me like a child

She uttered three words
No need to say anymore
My heart sank and I knew
It was true, I was sure

Together we cried floods
And I couldn't believe
After the great day I had
I was so naïve.

Kay Hughes (15)
Carmel RC College, Darlington

A Green Planet

A green planet would be great,
A green planet is what we need,
To help us grow,
To help us live,
A green planet would be great,
Stop polluting it,
You've gone mad,
Having a red planet would be bad,
A green planet would be great.

Jake Todhunter (11)
Carmel RC College, Darlington

13

Just Remember

Night turns to day,
Day turns to night.
Just remember,
It will all be over soon.

Sea turns to land,
Land turns to sea.
Just remember,
It will be gone.

Sun turns to moon,
Moon turns to sun.
Just remember,
Anything can change.

Sky turns to stars,
Stars turn to sky.
Just remember,
The times there were.

Life turns to death,
Death carries on.
Just remember,
What was said.

Rebecca Barr (13)
Carmel RC College, Darlington

Dreams

The future belongs to those who believe in the beauty of their
dreams, no matter what it seems,
so you might be on the right track to developing your dreams,
but you'll get run over if you just sit there doing nothing.

Anyone can make their dreams come true,
if they have the courage to pursue them,
no matter what anyone will say or do,
just know in your heart your dreams can come true.

Hannah Boyce (12)
Carmel RC College, Darlington

14

Life

Live life to the full,
Make the most of what you can.
Death is getting closer
And waiting for you to come.

Every minute is going by,
So don't dwell on the past.
Everyone has a brighter future,
So make the most of what you can.

Care about others,
And they'll care about you.
Every time you love them,
They'll love you too.

Make life as fun as you can
And make the most of now.
Don't take things for granted
And cherish the memories you've got.

Every time you think about others,
They'll think about you.
Don't miss an opportunity,
So live life to the full.

Jagjven Kaur (14)
Carmel RC College, Darlington

My Poem

Walkers of day walked into the night,
People running for their next flight,
Beautiful things all around,
Always hearing a lovely sound,
People driving up the street,
People having friends to meet,
And then when the day is over now,
Nobody makes a sound.

Dean Pallister (12)
Carmel RC College, Darlington

15

Art Thou An Angel!

The word love,
Is a powerful thing,
As you move like a graceful dove,
You step out of that shimmering veil,
And I had a natural thought,
It's an angel! Should I hail?

As long as the sun sets
And the moon rises,
The Heavens will sing just for you.
For as long as I love, and the love that I give,
A sweet robin, for only you it will coo.
For your beauty is such a divine image,
That only thy deepest thought
Could dream of.

As stones taught me to fly,
My love for you taught me to lie.
And that life taught me to cry,
But you know, that I just
Don't
Know . . .

Dominic Gay (12)
Carmel RC College, Darlington

Helpless!

She heard her heart shatter into a million pieces,
As he walked away and left her crying,
She tried to stop him but he kept going and going,
She watched, helpless.
Helpless she watched, she knew nothing she could say would make
him stop,
She thought back, remembering their friendship before he kissed her,
Just thinking about it made her cry, even after everything,
Knowing she would never again hear his voice,
She watched him walk around the corner and out of her life forever!

Rachel Miller (13)
Carmel RC College, Darlington

16

My Mum

My mum is amazing!
She can always tell when there is something wrong
and never gets tired of saying, 'I love you'
She comforts me
spoils me
and cares for me 24 hours a day

Shopping sprees are the best with her
She always knows what looks good on me
and if she sees something
that is just me
I am sure to find it waiting on my bed
always making me feel special

Sundays are a meal out
and a walk with our four dogs
through the miles of greenery
all the great days out
with my mum
one-off she is!

Holly Armitstead (13)
Carmel RC College, Darlington

You

My world was in dark,
Until then, there, a bright spark.

You are my brightest light,
When I saw you, my life reached its height.

As I lie in bed,
You're still in my head.

All I do is think about you,
I don't know what to say, you're too good to be true.

When I see you my mind goes fuzzy,
You're a million times sweeter than a piece of candy.

Lewis Malcolm (13)
Carmel RC College, Darlington

17

Something I've Got To Find . . .

As the silver stars glistened,
They brightened up the jet-black sky.
I made hearts in the stars,
As my eyes twinkled in the darkness.

I lay on some leaves,
And in amongst dry sand,
I could hear the sea crashing,
As my eyes twinkled in the darkness.

Suddenly lightning bolts stabbed around me,
But they seemed to miss my terrified body,
I hoped for help from the sky,
As my eyes twinkled in the darkness.

It was almost like God had seen me suffer,
Before I had any time to blink,
I was back in my old bungalow, I think
As eyes twinkled in the darkness.

I found my heart's desire.

Charlotte Bowe (13)
Carmel RC College, Darlington

Family

Family is a brilliant thing
Mum, Dad, brothers, sisters and pets too
Little kids wingeing all day long
Stroppy teenagers with nothing to do
Family is a brilliant thing

Family is a brilliant thing
Helping with homework
Screaming at the kids
Doing all the washing up
Family is a brilliant thing.

Erin Graham (11)
Carmel RC College, Darlington

Life

I have learnt all I need to know in life,
That you do not need to be loved to be happy, you just need really good friends.
That no matter what you tell your mam or dad, they will listen to you,
You do not need a mam and dad to have a family.
You do not need to be rich to have friends, good friends are always there.
Everybody is the same, even if they look different,
They are the same if they have a disability or follow another religion.

And just because one person does not like somebody, does not mean you have to dislike them.
You can learn all you need to know in life at 12 so why are people bullied for being poor,
Or not having a mam or dad,
Or being disabled,
Or having another religion?

Courtney Armstrong (12)
Carmel RC College, Darlington

Crash

I was going to do well
This was my day
All I was doing was singing hooray, hooray!
Speeding by with no care
See why would I when I was nearly there?
Rustle, rustle to my surprise, what was that?
I could not believe my eyes
Bang, whack, I hit my head
Going into the trees full speed ahead
I could not stop you see, no, no what could I do?
Black
Yes, this was my day, hooray, hooray!
I could never walk again. Oh yes, I was on my way.

Amarachi Duru (13)
Carmel RC College, Darlington

19

From The Darkness

It was coming from the darkness,
I could see the shadow,
I swallowed and took a breath,
It was coming out of the darkness.

It was coming out of the darkness,
I could see the outline of a person,
I swallowed and took a breath,
I stepped out of the darkness.

It stepped out of the darkness,
I could see arms, legs and a face,
I swallowed and took a breath,
It stepped towards me.

It stepped towards me,
I saw its mouth open,
It swallowed and I took my last breath.

Lucy Hull (12)
Carmel RC College, Darlington

Love Will Fight

We look, we stare, we fall
Our eyes meet and we feel the heat
I love you, as you love me
We are true and shall live life through
Does your heart beat like mine does?
Does it skip a beat every time we meet?
Suddenly I feel an underlying wish
To spend my life with you until the parting time of death
I will not rest, I will not give
Until you're with me, until I'm yours
We will be best, we will be sweet
    We will be the ones
    Who are the perfect match.

Emma Shackleston(13)
Carmel RC College, Darlington

The Cheshire Cat From Alice's Point Of View

The Cheshire cat is not a pet breed,
He has pink and purple stripes and sings Jabberwocky songs.
He appears out of nowhere, and all you can hear is his voice.
His only giveaway is his white shiny teeth, smiling at you
in the darkness.
I met this queer cat when walking alone on a path,
as he was watching me from his tree.
He told me he belonged to a Duchess, who was the first person
I met on my travels. '
I call him the grinning cat for his mischievous ways,
in addition to his vanishing acts.
His big, yellow eyes are always watching you, and you never
know what he is going to do next . . .
That's what you need to watch out for if you ever meet
the grinning cat
Whilst walking in Wonderland.

Lauren Davis (12)
Carmel RC College, Darlington

Remembrance Day

The day the soldiers died
they died with honour and pride.

The day the poppies grew
they grew in remembrance of you.

The day when all emotion had gone
was the day millions of loved ones mourned.

The day when the last bullet was shot
was the day the great war ended.

The day when the remaining soldiers
stood with pride and respect to collect their medals of bravery
was the day I gave a sigh of relief.

Harriet Ashley (12)
Carmel RC College, Darlington

21

The Amazing Day

I love London, it's so amazing
Sometimes I do gown there racing
I turn the corner, I speed the straight
But when there's a slow guy I have to wait.

Finally I make my move
I speed past him, I'm in my groove
I'm coming up to my last lap
I really feel like giving someone a slap.

I'm really nervous but I'm feeling great,
The finish line's coming, I can't wait.

I cross the line, I hear a cheer
I get out of my cart and get popped a beer
I'm on the podium, I'm on the top
This day is great, I like it a lot.

Costner Brown (13)
Carmel RC College, Darlington

The Waiting

As I was waiting on a very hot day
Waiting for the visitor
I heard someone running
Running more
I turned around to look at the door
Bang! Bang! Bang! Who could it be?
Was it the visitor or was it just me?
Should I open it? 'Cause I'm going to
Argh! Boo! As the cool breeze passed
I realised it was my friend from Poole
I said, 'Why run?'
He said, 'The visitor, are you ready?'
He is late
It must just be fate
He was meant to meet me at eight!

Joseph Austin (12)
Carmel RC College, Darlington

22

Memories

I can remember the days we used to laugh and cry.
The memories we've shared and the day you died.
I know that you wouldn't want to go like this
And I wished I could have given you that goodnight kiss.
If this is what life has to give, why are the bad ones the ones that live?
I guess that he's running out of angels up there,
So he took you as you were the only one that cares.
You've been there from the beginning to the very end
And I know one thing for sure, you'll always be my best friend.

Elle-Jo Brown (13)
Carmel RC College, Darlington

Thinking Of You

You're all that's on my mind,
Please just save me from your eyes,
They lock my heart inside,
I wish I was with you all the time,
I miss the person you were before,
I loved you more and more and more,
Then less,
When I got that call, you had kissed that girl,
My heart it fell, I couldn't talk,
My friends they said I deserved more.

Eleanor McAllister (13)
Carmel RC College, Darlington

23

Nothing Lasts Forever

That startling smile
Your voice so calm
Each freckle where it's supposed to be

Your eyes so bright
Hands so rough
A laugh that makes me smile

You're my everything
You're my nothing
If nothing lasts forever.

Abi Allan (13)
Carmel RC College, Darlington

Emotions

The emotion love, passion, desire,
Hatred, jealousy, raging and fire.
The emotion sad, upset and sorrow,
The emotion lonely, making you feel hollow.
The emotion petrified, fear, scared,
The emotion embarrassed, you have only just bared.
The emotion excited, happy, ecstatic,
These are my emotions, I'm not that dramatic.

Ben Joyeux (13)
Carmel RC College, Darlington

Valentine's Day

Valentine's Day some people love it, some people like it, but who
would, the day that your best friend . . .
I don't have to say any more
Valentine's Day isn't about being happy
It's about love and my love
For my friend
May he rest in peace.

Charlotte Curry (13)
Carmel RC College, Darlington

My Poem

Cardiff City who play in blue,
they are the best,
better than all the rest,
they are so immense,
and when they play they create suspense.

Cardiff City who play in blue,
Cardiff City play like a team,
they make it look like a dream,
Cardiff City are so great,
they decide their own fate.

Cardiff City who play in blue,
they pass it out wide,
then back to the other side.
Cardiff City make every tackle,
it is worth the hustle.

Amandeep Singh Buttar (13)
Cwmcarn High School, Newport

David And Goliath

David and Goliath was not fair,
But not as unfair
As the sloppy pair
Named Tom and Clair,
They eat pear
When on a chair.

They tell the time,
Lemon and lime,
The swine,
He should be covered in slime,
But that pine . . .
Tree,
Was like a hairy bee,
Playing on the Wii.

Alex Spencer (13)
Cwmcarn High School, Newport

25

Reflecting Hope

Hope dies,
Liquid dreams shattered on the broken hearts, built on heartless lies.

Rainbows, disused and rainless, shatter on concrete,
There's no rainbow without rain, no hope without pain.

It lies,
A single gem, more precious, more priceless, but unable to be bought.

It falls. Alive for a second, a clear flow, so visible, so colourless,
And falls. A crystal drop, a mirror into an inner world.

A childhood lost, a love now gone and dead,
A happier day, a silent prayer, no rest for the wearied head.

One drop, two drop, three drop.

A silver drop giving one more hope that the world might care. One day

The sunlight glitters rainbow on it, reflecting, it glitters. It shines red and orange, yellow and green, blue and purple

Like jewels. They combine to a golden glimmer.
But it's too far to the end, make dreams come true.

All isn't dead, one more hope to the world it belongs to.
Before it dies. And fades.

Can we solidify dreams? One hope of his possibility,
In the silent silver sea, so small yet so big inside.

One drop, two drop, three drop.

The wings they spread only to be broken,
The doors they closed, now locked forever,
The times they tried, hopeless endeavour.

Can we measure dreams? Can we weigh sadness?
Yet something so weightless should contain so much.

Could a seed grow, watered by the salty rain?
In each is the taste of hopeless dreams, filled with hope.

26

It touches a life as it drips. To fall. To fizz. And fade.
One whole life in a single second.

Every joy and every pain, every hope and every fear.
Reflected in the precious rain, reflected by a single tear.

Bethan Thomas (14)
Cwmcarn High School, Newport

Forever

Forever and a day,
That's all you hear me say,
I'll love you forever,
Forever and a day.

You're laughing on a rainbow,
You're dancing on the clouds,
You're singing on the sunshine
And it's clear and loud.

You're vast like an ocean,
You're free like a dove,
When I think of happy memories,
It's then I feel your love.

Now you're shining with radiance,
You're shining in the sky,
Like a beautiful butterfly,
Keep on flying high.

You're the light that lights my life,
The spark of ignition within me,
You're my inspiration and hope
And there'll always be a *we*.

Forever and a day,
That's all you hear me say,
I'll love you forever,
Forever and a day.

Nadia Yamamoto
Cwmcarn High School, Newport

Social Battleground

There is a place where people fight and battle,
The rounds going rattle, rattle,
And the tacticians going nattle, nattle,
I had just connected to the game.

The confident, aggressive melee-ing ones,
The light machine gun mag emptying ones,
And the sit and wait for you to pass by ones,
Had just connected to the game.

The ones playing all night - if they can cope,
The snipers that need no scope,
And that twitty swearing dope,
Had just connected to the game.

The running and hiding scaredy-cats,
The mean and bullying cyber rats,
And all those who just want a chat,
Had just connected to the game.

The pros that dominate the map,
The American in a baseball cap,
And the ones who set a claymore trap,
Had just connected to the game.

The ones whose tactics are as perfect as cubes,
The ones that use grenade launching tubes,
And the ones who are plainly noobs,
Had just connected to the game.

The ones who stir up a mighty thrill,
The ones who like to spawn kill,
And the ones who escape and over the hill,
Had just connected to the game.
A place for everyone,
Modern Warfare 2.

Alistair Davies (13)
Cwmcarn High School, Newport

28

Home You'll Fly

The day has come,
He's supposed to be at work,
He's supposed to walk through
That door in a few days' time.

Except the fact that he
Was carried home yesterday,
In his personalised box.

The kids so grief stricken,
The wife is lost,
The family has lost.

No letter had come through the post
That week, just a letter
Explaining that he's not walking home.

The tears they shed each night and day,
Just a symbol for many in this world today,
The fighting does not stop,
Even though you've gone.

The kids in tears,
The wife in tears,
The parents have a missing child.

This sight is too familiar,
For the world to now forget,
200 lost on minimum,
With no chance of coming back.

So home you'll fly,
In your special box,
Flowers now cover you,
Just they wish
They could have said goodbye.

Jessica Hardaker (15)
Cwmcarn High School, Newport

The Lost Bag

The link, the foyer and form, I can't take it anymore,
I've lost my bag,
I can't think where,
In the link, the foyer and form!

The gym, outside and upstairs, I can't find it anywhere,
The LRC,
And the sports hall,
In the gym, outside and upstairs!

Last lesson was history, I asked Mr Regulski,
All he saw was
Me on my phone
In last lesson history!

Science was the lesson before, I asked Dr Wray as well,
'Checked your form room?'
Miss suggested
In science, the lesson before!

My form tutor, Mrs Smith, suggested the changing rooms,
But my peer,
Megan S said,
She saw it outside the link!

I'm certain I checked out there, so maybe I didn't look
Thoroughly, but,
I'll check again,
I really hope it's out there!

Yes! It's there! Oh that's great, I can't believe I missed it,
Must have had my
Head in the clouds,
Now to English, oh great, I'm late!

Chloe Johnson (12)
Cwmcarn High School, Newport

The Lala Land

In the Lala Land lie overpaid humans with a special thing,
Full of spoilt teenagers and music bands who cannot sing.
In the Lala Land they do what they please,
They can get their slaves to clean up, even when they sneeze.
In the Lala Land are men who kick a ball around a field,
But they get paid billions once that contract deal is sealed.
In the Lala Land cameras watch your every move,
Even in the shower when you're singing to that groove.
In the Lala Land these humans act like birds,
Always tweet, tweet, tweeting to those clones
who come in herds.
In the Lala Land they make our life full of talk,
Always complaining about gaining the extra pound
from taking that cake off the fork.
In the Lala Land they take over our TVs,
And some of them even making successful CDs.
In the Lala Land are humans full of energy,
Who like to dance to that club hit remedy.
In the Lala Land are people with big mansions
and a swimming pool,
But they don't think it's even just that cool.
In the Lala Land they're just like me and you,
Except they can push in, in that big roller coaster queue.
Everyone wants to be in the Lala Land some day,
But unlike them we'll work hard to find our own way!

Alice Matthews (13)
Cwmcarn High School, Newport

The Beach - Haiku

Golden sand glistens
Huge waves crash on the seashore
Deep sea shimmering.

Cameron Greenslade (12)
Cwmcarn High School, Newport

31

Summer

When the grass grows high,
Pointing towards the cloudless sky,
When the sun beats down,
Upon the sprawling town,
When the trees drift lazily,
And the grass is full of daisies,
When you feel free,
Unbound for eternity,
When I feel trapped,
Lost in the past,
When you're on the beach,
Fun is not something you teach.

For me,
Life is a memory,
But summer brings back more,
When I remember about the others,
Upon the other shore.

Summer is fun,
Yes, I'll admit it!
With flowers, holidays and all the sun,
But sometimes I remember,
The ones that are gone,
I remember us laughing,
In the summer sun.

Regina Ansell (11)
Cwmcarn High School, Newport

Bananas!

Bananas give you a buzz
With their bright yellow fuzz
Nutritious and sweet
Delicious to eat
Amazing and stunning
The treat that will keep you running!

Megan Samuel (11)
Cwmcarn High School, Newport

32

Ever-Flowing River

River's mouth overflows
A trickle of water
Escapes

Its dark, gloomy
And mysterious
Colour flows with the
Atmosphere around

It's reflected in the moonlight
The temptation, desperation is
Greater as the journey goes on

It's alone
Lost in darkness around

Continuously flowing
Through the forest
Without any sound

Coming to an end
It reaches its peak

Throws itself off

And lands at the bottom
Where it began.

Charlotte Watkins (18)
Cwmcarn High School, Newport

My Poem

Chocolate and sweets
Like bed sheets
Likes his meat
Wait, he's a veggie
Kieran Harrison
Cousin Reggie
What a wedgie!

Harvey Reader (13)
Cwmcarn High School, Newport

The City Under The Sea

Deep below the Atlantic surface,
Lies a city with no purpose.
With water in every inch and square,
Powerful Poseidon would not even dare to go there.

The blue, barbaric city dwellers are as evil as can be,
They hang their enemy's heads on a beautiful coral tree.
No one knows of them except you and I,
Never ever go there, for you will surely die.

Their houses are made of plain, dull brick, unlike ours,
Time works differently there, they don't have seconds, minutes or hours.
Their houses have no doors because they do not steal,
But they are not friendly, they eat each other for every meal.

Their super, spectacular knowledge of design, is like no other,
That's why they've never been found, they're always undercover.
They tried to make it beautiful, but failed miserably,
They couldn't find anything wrong with it and so they could not see.

Now you know of the story, of the city under the sea,
I have another story to tell, so will you listen with me?
But for now it's farewell from me, one and all,
Oh, and if you see the meaning of this story, go on, give us a call.

Joel Haines (12)
Cwmcarn High School, Newport

My Poem

Chelsea will never win the League,
Ha, ha, ha, ha, ha, ha, ha, ha, ha.
Every player has fatigue,
La, la, la, la, la, la, la, la, la.
So you know Man U will win all the way,
Even if Chelsea try, hey, hey!
And Man U have lots of trophies
But Chelsea have very li-tt-le!

Joshua Gadd (12)
Cwmcarn High School, Newport

 34

The Bomb

A bomber plane flies overhead,
Carrying a cargo of dread.
High above the city it flies,
Bringing death to the skies.

Below the people walk so free,
Unaware that they should flee.
A mother and child are having fun,
Oblivious that their time has come.

The crew in the plane release the thing,
Knowing the devastation it will bring.
An awful moment must pass,
For now they must fly, fast.

Behind them there is a catastrophe,
As every human, bird and tree,
Gets caught in a burning cloud of smoke,
But they die before they can choke.

In the once busy city,
The streets are now filled with pity,
As high above them floating like a kite,
A mushroom cloud is the only sight,
An iconic reminder of the bomb.

Kelly Astley-Jones (13)
Cwmcarn High School, Newport

Mirror Girl

I enter my room
and she is there,
I can fly,
stand and stare.
There she sits upon my bed,
side to side, she turns her head.
I look again, what do I see?
It's only a mirror and in it is me!

Chelsie Bristow (13)
Cwmcarn High School, Newport

The Circus

The children laughed,
The toddlers cried,
The mothers talked,
The fathers sighed.

The rides screeched,
The balloons went pop!
The speakers boomed,
The ice cream went plop!

The lion roared,
The tiger grumbled,
The children squealed,
The parents mumbled.

The popcorn popped,
The peanuts crunched,
The parents sighed,
The children munched.

The circus was in town,
The children were excited,
The teenagers weren't happy,
They wish they weren't invited!

Morgan-Rose Young (13)
Cwmcarn High School, Newport

Autumn

As the leaves fall off the trees
As a breeze whistles like a train
Through the middle of my fingers
Frost lies on our cars all night
The wind makes a tornado of leaves
All the fires are in homes
Keeping the coldness out
As summer dies away
Autumn hits us hard.

Liam Moore (12)
Cwmcarn High School, Newport

36

Why Me?

It happens almost every day,
I cannot stand it,
Make it go away,
Close your eyes and you will see,
All the damage you have done to me.

I think to myself, *there is no fear*,
So I will wipe that silent tear,
Look at me and you will see,
That all I'm doing
Is just being me!

Someday I will not try,
I will just break down and cry,
I ignore their remarks,
They're just a bunch of sharks,
Hoping to kill me inside.

All you do is tell me this and tell me that,
You call me a brat and also fat,
But won't you just leave me alone,
And let me handle my life on my own?
I'm just fed up of being a nobody.

Courtney John (12)
Cwmcarn High School, Newport

Chelsea FC

C hampions
H ere
E ver
L iving
S laying
E very
A mbitious

F ootball
C lub.

Jack Dunn (13)
Cwmcarn High School, Newport

37

Sporting Dreams

Trying to be the best,
Targets and goals keep on rising,
Fighting for that sporting dream.

Training five days a week,
With no free time,
No time for parties or socialising.

Many competitions all over the country,
From local to British,
To international.

Many friends I have, all different ages,
Lots of nice coaches,
One's even met the Queen.

Conditioning, conditioning,
Fitness is a must,
Anything to be on top.

From acrobatic to artistic
And even tumbling,
Will my name be in lights
For the Olympic team?

Kira Sparkes (12)
Cwmcarn High School, Newport

Vampires

The newborns always come back,
They never ever hit the sack,
Golden eyes from red to black,
Gorgeous, graceful bloodsuckers.

Some say they have no heart,
Their humble families hardly part,
They all run as fast as darts,
Gorgeous, graceful bloodsuckers.

Abi Richards-Anning (13)
Cwmcarn High School, Newport

Jealousy

Jealousy, jealousy
It should be a crime
Jealousy, jealousy
It happens all the time

It's a terrible feeling
I can hardly fight it
My mind is unpeeling
I really don't like it
What is happening? What is the plot?
My friendship's unwrapping I want it to stop!

What if I'm not quiet?
What if I'm too loud?
I'm not very shy
I like to fit in with the crowd

I want to beat this feeling so bad
It's making me feel so bad and sad
I'll fight with all my might
I'll try to put up a greater fight.

Jodie Williams (13)
Cwmcarn High School, Newport

Reflection

There I sit on my chair
Looking at her long brown hair
She looks back with dark brown eyes
As round as those pork pies.

She sits there no movement at all
Standing strong and looking tall
I wonder who it is? Is it me?
That's the reflection in the mirror I see!

Emily Penson (13)
Cwmcarn High School, Newport

39

The Tree!

The ever looming Ent,
Giant staring down at me,
Brown with a green afro.
The tree.

He follows me around wherever I may go
Except inside, but he is always there
By the window.
The tree.

He makes a great hiding spot, up in-between the branches,
He's also a great bodyguard,
One that never deserts,
For I can see him always,
With his bright green afro.
The Tree.

Me and my mates may not always be mates,
But my tree is a friend for life,
If I'm feeling down, he's the one with the huge green crown.
The Tree.

Lloyd Gronow (13)
Cwmcarn High School, Newport

My Poem About Football

Football is one of many sports,
You can run around in your stretchy shorts.
You kick and pass and score a goal,
Sometimes it'll hit a white pole.
There's an attacker, a defender, and midfielders too,
Top of the league is the best position,
Until you lose and miss one shot,
Then you'll go from top to bot.

Luke Harris (12)
Cwmcarn High School, Newport

40

Immortal Life

A vision of beauty,
A magical creature,
He entered my life
And now I won't let him leave it.

There could never be another,
Who could take your place,
The beauty of your jet-black eyes,
The beauty of your stone-cold face.

He said he loved me,
He said I was the one,
And at the least expected moment,
He broke my heart.

He stepped forward and whispered to my neck,
The vampire bites,
The victim dies,
This death cannot be forever,
Immortal life.

Alis Stone (13)
Cwmcarn High School, Newport

The Stalking Ghost Of Cwmcarn High School

She came to Cwmcarn High School,
With a pale face and devil eyes,
With an evil look,
That said, 'I will never say my byes!'

She looked as pale as winter snow,
Drifting to the ground,
Sad and lonely with no friends,
Her lonely footsteps walked around!

Doesn't anyone know she's there?
Shall I ask my friends, do they see her
Or do they see nothing
But a blur?

I thought I would take the chance and ask.
But the lonely girl only said,
'I am not noticed, you only notice me,
You should know, I am a stalker who is dead!'

Hannah Green (13)
Cwmcarn High School, Newport

The Welsh Dragon!

There once was a dragon called Fred
who lived in a very big shed
He huffed and puffed with all his might
and smoked up a great big light.

In the small valleys where Fred liked to stay
he goes out with his friends just to play
Fred loves to eat at Pizza Hut
but he doesn't like it when it's shut.

Fred is a very happy dragon
and loves to visit St Fagan's
Which is where he learns about history
and unravels a Welsh mystery.

Leah-Marie Hill (13)
Cwmcarn High School, Newport

42

Sea Dreams

Wetsuit on with life vest too,
Goggles, gloves and rubber shoes.
Climb aboard and off we go,
Inflatable 'hell bent' in tow.

Through the waves we rise and dip,
Wet with spray from hair to hip.
Flapping hair and face aglow,
Happy smiles on full show.

I love to see the Cornish coast,
Fish and birds but seals the most.
With bobbing heads and whiskers too,
Sunbathing on rocks but shying from view.

How fast the day does pass at sea,
And now my bed is calling me.
Peel my wetsuit, have my tea,
Shower, bed and dream of the sea.

Megan Bateman (11)
Cwmcarn High School, Newport

Friends

They warm you when you're cold
and they hug you when you're sad,
they are there for you to hold,
they love you even when they're mad.

They talk to you when you're alone,
when you're down they make you smile,
they put up with you when you moan,
for you they'd run the extra mile.

Your friends are more like your family
and they help you through the strife,
you keep your friends forever,
you keep your friends for life.

Megan Mellish (12)
Cwmcarn High School, Newport

43

The Coalition Of 2010

Working hand in hand,
To meet the country's demand,
Making that difficult decision,
To work together in a coalition.

Two teams moulded into one,
To decide how the country's run,
They pull together as a team,
Strong and defiant they must be seen.

Working on the economy,
For a better future for you and me,
An on-going battle,
That they strive to tackle.

Clegg and Cameron are their names,
In 2010 they came to fame,
Now we watch them every day,
And for wrong decisions we will pay.

Bethan Winterson (13)
Cwmcarn High School, Newport

Abandoned House

A house is calling for someone to enter,
No one inside but a whistle from the wind,
No boats on the shore,
No one goes near.

No smoke enters the air,
No animals live there,
Ivy crawls up the walls,
No one goes near.

Windows boarded up,
Heather on the roof,
Slime on the door,
No one goes near.

Caitlin Tyler (12)
Cwmcarn High School, Newport

Talking Dogs
(A poem in the style of Benjamin Zephaniah)

Be nice to yu dogs dis Easter
Cos dogs just wanna ave fun bones
Dogs are cute an are small
An every dog has a home
Be nice to yu dogs dis Easter
Dey wanna ave fun
Dey wanna enjoy it, they don't wanna hav a poorly tum.

Kathryn Bradley (11)
Daniels Tutoring, Blackpool

Friends

Friends are friends no matter what,
Even if they are a geek
Or a popular swat.

Some could be blonde or brunette,
With goofy teeth or glasses,
These sort of friends are hard to forget
And they don't grass you up in classes.

They could be skinny or they could be fat,
With short ginger hair,
But never say they're ginger,
Because that will upset them,
So call them strawberry blonde to be fair.

Most of my friends are quite weird,
But they are still my friends.
One of my friends has a beard,
(My dad) but they are still friends to the end.

Friends are friends no matter what,
Even if they are a geek,
Or a popular swat,
Friends are friends no matter what.

Emma Shearer (12)
Holy Cross Catholic High School, Chorley

My Home Town, Chorley

Chorley is amazing and perfect in every way,
It's clean and picturesque,
With rain pouring every day.

Chorley hates nature except for Astley Park,
There are lots of species to behold
When light turns into dark.

In the centre of the village lie the market stalls,
But if you've got expensive tastes
Then try the Preston malls.

Chorley's household prices are within an easy reach,
Employment knows no bounds,
You could build or sell or teach.

If you like to be outdoors
Then shopping streets are awaiting you,
But if shops are not your forté
Then Rivington is superb too.

Chorley is a busy place and links are not too far,
You can access it from anywhere,
By bus or rail or car.

For me the most fantastic place is my Chorley house,
My family have grown up right here
And never seen a mouse.

Chorley is the place we love,
To join us we do beckon,
If you come and join this town,
You'll love it we do reckon.

My home town is amazing,
In fact it's perfect in every way,
It's clean and picturesque,
The sun has just come out today.

Rebecca Coates (12)
Holy Cross Catholic High School, Chorley

46

My Dream

My mother told me once,
That dreams do come true.
So I sat there thinking
Of what I wanted to do.

I thought about a musician,
And then I thought about a rhyme.
But in the end I thought
I just wouldn't have the time.

Next I thought about a comedian,
And then I thought I'd write.
But then again it would be fun,
So then I thought I might.

In the end I said I'd wait
To find all of my dreams.
It could be easy and it could be hard,
But it's better than it seems.

So now I'll think I'll tell my mum,
That she might be right.
Oh wait, I think I've got it,
I'll reveal it tomorrow night . . .

Lauren Walmsley (12)
Holy Cross Catholic High School, Chorley

47

Behind A Mask

I have always been the one people came to for support . . .
For advice.
The one that people could talk to when they were down,
And in need of cheering up.
The one that people could confess their problems to,
Expecting I would fix them.
The one that people could spill out their secrets to,
And assume I would keep them.
The one that people could be at their most vulnerable in front of,
Knowing I would never take advantage of them.

For as long as I can remember
I have been there for the people around me . . .
A helping hand,
A problem solver,
A friend . . .
The whole time wearing a mask.
I have never let anyone know my true thoughts and feelings . . .
Let them get to know the real me!
For fear of them breaking me from the inside.
I have never let anyone close,
For fear of being hurt.
People who claim to know everything about me,
Actually know next to nothing.
They believe the mask . . .
What they see on the exterior,
Not delving any deeper.
Maybe if they tried searching, they would see . . .
See the pain submerged in my eyes,
And maybe they would wonder.

They have no idea about the burdens I bear,
The secrets that I keep,
That could so easily destroy the artificial peace around them.
They have no idea how much it hurts,
Knowing the things I do,
And not trusting a single soul.
They think that their problems are the most important things in the world,

Whilst pouring them out to anyone diligent enough to listen,
But they have no idea.
They haven't got a clue about the horrors that surround them,
Things that they pass every day,
But are not perceptive enough to see.

I could tell them . . .
Enlighten them.
I could ruin the little charade that they call life,
And bring their perfect world crashing and burning down around
them . . .
But I can't.
I suffer in silence,
Knowing the heartbreak and chaos I could cause.
The secrets that I know would shock them . . .
Horrify them,
And who knows who they would tell?

You know that old saying, 'A problem shared is a problem halved'?
Well, it isn't true.
You can tell someone a secret, and ask them to keep it,
But they will somehow let it slip, and tell someone else,
Who will then tell someone else,
And before long, everybody knows.
The secrets you were trusted with are no longer unknown,
And you are no longer trusted.

No, a problem shared is not a problem halved,
It is a problem doubled . . .
Trebled . . .
Quadrupled!
No, it is better to keep it to yourself,
And let it tear you apart from the inside slowly and painfully,
The pain of shame, upon the people you care about.

I have always been the strong one . . .
The one people depended on in their time of need.
The one that never let their emotions hinder them.
The one that kept their cool at all times,
No matter what the situation.
But what if I don't want to be that person anymore?
What if I want to go to someone else for support?

49

And not be the one giving it?
What if I want to talk to someone freely,
With no fear of betrayal?
What if I want to let my guard down,
Without feeling nervous and on edge, anticipating an attack?
I want to tell my secrets to someone,
Without fearing the consequences.
I don't want to be the one everyone else relies on anymore.
I want to be free.

Nikita Schaap (14)
Holy Cross Catholic High School, Chorley

Love Poem

Your words are sweet
Your words are fine
Your voice is divine
Call me sometime

Your face is pretty
Your face is neat
People are staring at you on the corner of the street

Your hair is brown
You're going down town
At quarter to seven
Kind like Heaven

Hell Kitty
Your name is so pretty
Your smile is so small
Your hair is so high
Butterflies are watching you in the dark sky.
Night!

Jordan Thomas (12)
Holy Cross Catholic High School, Chorley

The Show

Red lights, blue lights,
They flash across the stage.
Like butterflies fluttering,
From place to place.

It's my time now,
I must proceed,
Can you see the audience?
They're waiting for me!

Gulping, I step forward,
Teasing my cheesiest smile.
The stage is my only oyster,
The people, my crowd.

I sway through the music,
Reciting my lines,
Like pinned up puppets
I have them hooked,
They watch with saucepan eyes.

My words reach out,
Hitting the audience,
I know I'm meant for this!
The nerves are coming to rattle my legs,
So I squeeze my trembling fists.

Enthusiastically they clap,
Just as the music dies down,
We all gather together,
Grinning gleefully, we bow.

Rosie Pemberton (14)
Holy Cross Catholic High School, Chorley

51

Even Though You Can't Hear Me . . .

You may not be able to hear me,
But I have many things to say,
One is that I love you,
I miss you every day,

You always made me laugh,
You always cheered me up,
It's hard that you can't now,
It's like I have fallen in a giant dump.

You saved my life,
Didn't think of yours,
You always thought of others,
Look where it's got you now!

We pray for you every day,
Also every single night,
At the table and in the church,
Even at the place where you got hurt.

When you went it made a hole
In our lives and in our heart,
You were a massive thing in our lives,
You played a giant part.

Now that you have gone,
I don't know what to do,
You are all anyone thinks about,
I definitely always think about you.

So all I want to say, is that
I miss you every day,
I am so grateful for what you did,
I thank you all the time.

Alexandra Ellison (12)
Holy Cross Catholic High School, Chorley

Oh Grandpa

'Things were better when I was young,
The grass was greener,
The sky was bluer.
You could leave your front door open all day long,
No one would steal your possessions.
There was no terror threat,
You could walk the streets safe at night.
People used to talk to each other,
Neighbours looked after each other,
Things cost less to buy.'

'OK Grandpa, let me take in what you've said,
So things were different when you were younger.
The grass is still green,
The sky is still blue,
Not a lot of people had expensive possessions
So stealing was not an issue.
There was no terror threat, yes
But there were two world wars,
There were just as many murders
On the streets as there are now.
People still talk, Grandpa,
All over the world,
I can talk to my relatives in Australia
By the click of a button.
Things may have been cheaper,
But they were rationed and people went hungry.

I love you Grandpa and always will,
I will always listen to you.
I do feel pretty lucky in the world I live in today.'

Aimee Green (14)
Holy Cross Catholic High School, Chorley

53

Crazy Carnival!

Hooray!
It's the carnival day!
We made animals the theme,
The lion told us to,
He's really mean!

One child had to ask,
'Can I make a mask?'
The teacher said, 'Why not?
You've not asked for a lot.'

When we had finished the mask,
A boy went to ask,
'What about real animals in the zoo?
Can they come too?'

The teacher replied, 'Of course!
You can have a ride on a horse!'
The boy exclaimed, 'No! I want to be something funky!
Hey! I'll be a monkey!'

The parade started,
Pupils and animals darted!
Down the street,
Greeting everyone they did meet.

The music was playing loudly,
The children were walking proudly,
The animals were running wildly,
Carnival crazy!

The monkeys danced the jungle jig,
Followed by a laughing pig!
Then came the giraffe,
Sitting in a bath!

Now came the elephants,
Wearing some big pants.
'Look at the zebras galloping away,'
It looked like they'd had enough fun for today!

Huh, what's that?
It's the lion roaring,
He thinks this is all boring!
Now he's started snoring!

So we all went home,
But the hyenas were left licking a bone.
The monkeys went back to the zoo,
How about you?

Vito Esposito (12)
Holy Cross Catholic High School, Chorley

Whatever The Cost
(Dedicated to my family)

Whatever the cost,
They'll make a sacrifice,
To take me to a dance exam,
Instead of working twice.

Whatever the cost,
They'll do what they know's best,
To watch me at a netball match,
Instead of getting rest.

Whatever the cost,
They'll always be with me,
To help me with my homework,
Instead of making tea.

Bethany Wilson (12)
Holy Cross Catholic High School, Chorley

The Motor Race

I went to the motor race in town.
I was told my car was going down.
When I walked in I was amazed
Then I felt a bit dazed.

The boos, the hisses, the chants and the disses.
People said this was motor heaven and so did Dad's disses.
The cars got ready to race,
But then one of the drivers got hit by a pen.

The boom and crackles of the engines made people scream
But suddenly I was blinded by the car's gleam.
The race had started but not so well,
When one of the drivers leaned out the window and fell.

As the race was coming to an end
My car was coming round the last bend.
The two cars ricocheting off each other.
When my car won,
I hugged the driver, who was my brother.

Tony Simpson (12)
Irvine Royal Academy, Irvine

I'll Never Forget You

I'll never forget that day,
The day catastrophe trembled through my bones,
The day heartache depleted my body,
The day my world vanished into nothingness.

I'll never forget that wave,
The wave that prised you away from my clutches,
The wave that claimed millions including my love,
The wave that forced me to die inside.

I'll never forget the tears I shed,
The tears of a thousand weeping individuals,
The tears for my love, gone for evermore,
The tears streaming down my face, ongoing.

I'll never forget the memories,
The memories we shared through day and night,
The memories of the romance during our time side by side,
The memories of me saying these three words,

I love you.

Joshua Glennon (13)
John Ruskin School, Coniston

57

I Hold His Chart Firmly

I hold his chart firmly,
Dreading to turn the page.
Motion freezes.
Sound ceases.
I hold my breath,
My eyes scan the form.

No, not him,
Of all people.
The murderers, the thieves,
The terrorists.
This loving, ecstatic, peaceful man.
I couldn't do this to his family,
His friends, his colleagues.

I walk to his private room.
This room, now so cold.
So plain, so white, so ghostly.
This room, like an asylum cell.
How could it not drive a person mad?

He isn't looking at me
But gazing out the window.
'Please, open it.'
Surprised, I push the window open.
I would do anything to put this off.

The lump forms in my throat
But I force the words out.

I watch his face fall.
Then the birds stop singing,
The sun hides behind the clouds.
'I'm sorry, so sorry.'

Florence James (13)
John Ruskin School, Coniston

58

I Miss You

I remember your eyes
I remember your smile
I remember the day you left me
My heart got crushed
I miss you too much
No matter what I did
I cried and cried
I was five
Only five the day you died

Your blue overalls you took with you
Your oil printed cap belongs to me
Your memories mean heartache
Laughter and joy
All I can say is

I miss you

I remember your silly shepherds' pie
You made me when I was sad
You held me like I was the only person in the world
You made me feel so important and special

The fifteenth of June
Shocked the hearts
Of the Sawery family for life.

Lana McCarthy (13)
John Ruskin School, Coniston

I Need To Win . . .

I never knew this could be such fun!
But no time to say that -
I just need to run!

I passed a girl
who made me think (by the look on her face)
she needed a drink.

I've never had an award before;
so I'll try my best . . . but my legs are sore.

Just forget it. That'll be fine.
I need that trophy. I want it.
It's mine.

No one can take it away from me.
It's my dream now.
I want it to be.

I wish I was a kangaroo. I could jump so high.
Or maybe a bird - and then I could fly.

But no need for that. I'm in the lead.
I'm really thirsty.
It's water I need.

Now I am first. I can see the line.
Nothing can put me down.
I see the trophy. It's mine.

The finishing line is coming near.
Everyone's behind me, so close
I can smell their fear.

I've won! I have won!
It was hard, but such fun.

I have the trophy. It's in my hand.
Now I can hear
those screaming fans!

Niamh Hutton (12)
Larbert High School, Larbert

6o

The Big Race

On your marks!
Get set!
Go!

The wind is blowing in my face.
I know I'm going to win this race
but I really need to keep up pace.

Hurry, hurry! Don't stop now!
Nearly time to take a bow.

Keep on going -
nothing to it.
I need to run
so let's get through it.

I can't believe it! I've almost won.
I never expected
so much fun!

There's the trophy.
I know it's mine.
Quick! Quick! Over the line,

or someone will skip me
and I'll lose time.

Sophie D'Ambrosio (12)
Larbert High School, Larbert

61

The Grimmest Tale

Mirror, mirror, in the ivory frame,
Give my story a face and name.
Onyx hair and emerald eyes;
Rose red lips that draw sweet sighs.
I've tasted temptation in the form of fruit,
Felt the juice quench my long-parched throat.
Greed was my sin, but innocence my virtue.
Revenge was mine, in hot iron shoes.
Mirror, mirror, in the ivory frame,
Give my story a face and name.
Wicker basket and oaken hair;
Eyes as dark as the feral wolf's lair.
In my red cloak, I've stalked the forest green,
Tempting the beasts to indulge with my treats.
Lust was my sin, but virginity my virtue.
Revenge was mine, with a broken promise.
Mirror, mirror, in the ivory frame,
Give my story a face and name.
Slippers of glass, and gowns of gold;
Mine is a tale that is rarely told.
I worked so hard, and dressed like swine.
Who'd have thought I'd make my sisters blind?
Pride was my sin, but modesty my virtue.
Revenge was mine, with soulless doves.
Mirror, mirror, of shattered glass,
The story's been told of each bonny lass.
If this poem had some moral truth
It would be this, friend - beware the gilded youth.
The fairest maiden is Hell's guise of flesh -
Beware of the woman, with the sweetest caress.
She is the Eve that came before.
She is the doll, playing the whore.
She is the carrier of Man's greatest sin.
Revenge is a dish best served . . . feminine.

Stephanie Gallon (16)
Newcastle College, Newcastle upon Tyne

A Family Called Kenya

I look into the eyes of the poor and I feel their pain,
If anyone else were there too, I'm sure they'd feel the same.
Maasai children making their own home-made games,
We complain about the weather, they're lucky when it rains.

On the Equator, the large sun blazing like fire,
Sets behind Kilimanjaro, turns the sky from orange to sapphire.
No light pollution resulting in a solution
Of the Milky Way, galaxies and stars,
Without a telescope you can see Venus,
And sometimes you can see Mars.

Many different creatures roaming the vast land,
Some of which are endangered and require a helping hand.
The large, green and golden space ruled by the giant five,
Dominant and grand beasts making the most of their time alive.

The Kenyan people have a certain warmth and outgoing personality,
The type that would brighten up a situation of awkward banality.
Many peaceful, happy people make up their communities,
Then they come together,
To form one big family called Kenya in unity.

There's still a lot more to be said about this great nation,
A beautiful place full of creativity and variation.

Jasper Green (12)
Oakhill College, Clitheroe

Lessons

I'm sitting staring into space,
Not a thought in my head.
Bored out of my mind,
Wish I was in bed.

The teacher keeps on lecturing,
When will he stop?
The teacher keeps on talking,
When will he let it drop?

Then he sees me doodling,
And shouts across the room.
His voice ringing in my head,
I fear impending doom.

He stood me at the front,
And asked me what he'd said.
Then I start thinking,
Cogs turning in my head.

Why didn't I listen?
Should have paid attention!
I'm regretting it now,
Because I'm in detention!

Reece Moore (13)
Oakhill College, Clitheroe

I Hate, I Hate, I Hate

I hate when people eat with their mouths open.
I hate when people speak words just spoken.
I hate when people laugh at others' demise.
I hate when people tell lies.
I hate when people deprive others of fun.
I hate that people can kill with a gun.
I hate that people complain for no reason.
I hate that they complain about the weather, no matter what the season.
I hate that people tell you what you've done right or wrong.
I hate that people complain that you take too long.
I hate that people only care about money.
I hate that when you tell a joke they say you're not funny.
I hate that people don't think about their family and friends.
I hate that people say that your clothes aren't the new trend.
I hate some things, but I enjoy stuff too!
I enjoy the world and so should you!

Declan Acomb (12)
Oakhill College, Clitheroe

Homework

More homework I seem to shout,
What on Earth is that about?
I worked hard in class today.
Why do more at night? I say.

I sit and stare and daydream,
I think, what's that supposed to mean?
English finished, maths still left, I moan
I don't need homework, I can get by on my own.

I've still got lots of homework to do,
I wish I could do something new.
It's boring, but I have to do it.
It's detention if I miss a little bit.

Nathan Wenborn (12)
Oakhill College, Clitheroe

65

Football

Football is a sport,
Where we all should be treated the same.
But the men get all the money
And the men get all the fame.

We work as hard as they do,
To try and become the best,
But all the fans watch the boys play
And we're stuck with the rest.

Don't we deserve as much as them?
Life isn't fair!
We even play better football,
Doesn't anybody care?

Laura Ratcliffe (13)
Oakhill College, Clitheroe

Writer's Block

A pen lurks on the paper - ravenous for ink,
Expectant for her to perceive the question adrift in the air.
Instead she inhales the salty scent of the earth,
As dense droplets of moisture patter,
Mimicking athletes on a track.
Icy chills creep suspiciously up her trouser leg,
Resulting in a violent shiver passing through her spine.
An abrupt rustle of a midday train hurries by,
Yet her head remains persistently desolate,
Inspiration is sparse,
Is it all used up?
Too many people?
Too many verses?
Just blank paper - dampened by the rain,
And all in that moment she knows what to write.

Meg Long (12)
Penwortham Girls' High School, Preston

66

Dawn Cascade

The first light of dawn splintered the frozen skies,
Casting mellow orange shadows across the land.
From below came a fountain of whispering cries,
Flowing like water over the sand.

A spout of twinkling bubbles popped as they rose,
Sending sparkles of teardrop stars across the grass.
They settled soft on the blades wherever they chose,
Allowing the tides of time to pass.

Mantles of light arose from trickles of thought,
As a hot drift of syrupy shadows gurgled up.
The simmering fires of the chiming dawn, caught
Deep in the day's lemon-scented cup.

Prowling winds with sparkles of coconut air,
Like dark, rippling silk on a meandering road.
The cool, mildewed morning unfurled like a broad stair,
Engulfing the night's lethargic load.

Sofie Macdonald (14)
Portree High School, Portree

A Lass Frae Skye

There once was a lassie frae Skye
Who happened tae like a fair guy
He could play on the fiddle
He could write a gud riddle
But he couldnae cook a gud pie.

Eryn Shinnie (13)
Portree High School, Portree

Waterfall Of Time

The lilting call of the evening birds,
Fanned out into the deepening oily descent of dusk.
The leathery sound of a million fireflies,
Captured the day in a slumbering husk.

Dark, rippling satin enveloped the sky,
The prowling wind succumbing with the drooping sunrays.
The lethargic, sleepy light of the silver moon,
Whisked the shivering whispers in their separate ways.

A sprinkling of emerald voices,
Drifted lazily through the ambling night.
Shadows of forgotten words were the noises
That followed the stars in their flight.

The gurgle and chime of the scented air,
Cascaded down the staggering way.
At the end, the waking light dozed there,
Whipping up the dancing hours of the day.

Josephine Macdonald (14)
Portree High School, Portree

Dad

I had a dad
Who was bad
At being a lad

He's grown up now
He can eat a cow!
I don't know how

My dad is great
But he's sometimes late
But most importantly he's my mate.

Matthew King (13)
Queen Elizabeth's Grammar School, Blackburn

68

My Lovely Aunty Andrea

My aunty is happy
She is very yappy
She spoils me rotten
I think she's forgotten
That I'm not the only child

She gives me loads of chocolate
Quite a lot
My teeth will soon fall out
So many I can't count

She really cares for me
It's like I'm being stung by a bee
She looks after me so good
She would pull me out of the mud
If I fall into it
Just a little bit

My aunty is so kind
So much I don't mind
She gets me out of trouble
And gives me a good cuddle

Her dog is so cute
Not anything like a newt
Her dog cuddles me so close
It's like she's given me a love overdose

I can't believe she is my aunty
She is so bouncy
I'm happy I've got her
I just hope it stays that way.

Ellie Danson (12)
Queen Elizabeth's Grammar School, Blackburn

My Mum

My mum is really cool,
But amazingly not a fool.
She thinks she's very smart,
But she's not good in any art.

My mum is kind and caring,
Although a little daring.
She always tells me, 'Never give up,'
If I am in trouble or if I am stuck.

My mum is small but sweet,
She is precise and neat.
She is round and always curled,
I think she's the best in the world.

She hugs me and says how much she loves me,
She will always be there to protect me.
She says she will be with me wherever I go,
Her love growing for evermore.

She is always there for me,
Even when she doesn't need to be.
I trust her more than anything
And between us will come nothing.

My mum is a real treat
Whose memories will always be sweet.
She will always stay close to my heart,
Even when we are forced to depart.

Safeer Sheikh (12)
Queen Elizabeth's Grammar School, Blackburn

My Brother

My brother is a funny guy,
Stupid, he thinks he can fly.
He's only eleven,
But acts like seven.
He likes to eat with chopsticks,
He plays rugby, a lot of drop kicks.

Everybody says he's cute,
He talks so much I would put him on mute.
He's good at annoying people,
I think he's a heapful.
He makes origami,
This shape and that . . .
He can make a hippo or even a bat.

My brother is very nice at times,
He's useless at making poems that rhyme
But he's clever at making,
Amazing at baking.
He likes to cook
From a Delia Smith book.

He doesn't like veg,
His favourite movie is 'Over The Hedge'.
And that's all the time
For my brother,
You're like no other.

Dalen Chan (13)
Queen Elizabeth's Grammar School, Blackburn

Miscreants

Are you afraid of the miscreants?
They disobey and refuse to pay.
Their ignorance and persistence
Ruins children's innocence.

They are monotheistic,
Their god is violence.
They want defiance,
They don't want silence.

A man stands up in isolation,
He expresses his anger, pain and frustration.
He gets ignored,
His peers are bored.
They gave him promises,
He was assured.

We try to our optimum
To stop the dissidence.
But is it enough?
Are they too tough?

Great powers line a tower,
It's grand and tall,
What it does is far too small!

Gregory Mott (14)
Queen Elizabeth's Grammar School, Blackburn

My Dad Poem

This poem is about my dad,
He makes me feel glad.

He is never really sad,
But when it is my dad,
He always looks rad,
And my dad,
He has a dad
Who is my grandad,
And he never really had
A sad dad,
So my dad
Had a dad,
They were all mad,
When my dad was a lad,
He thought that his dad
Was a bit mad,
But I will never know his dad's dad,
So now I hope you know about my dad
And all the things he has ever had,
But there is just one thing,
Do you think I am mad?

James Quigley (13)
Queen Elizabeth's Grammar School, Blackburn

Manic Mum

'Don't do this, do that instead,
I've just mopped the floor,
So mind where you tread!'
Her usual orders as she walks out the door,
Her voice trailing off to be heard no more,
'Have you fed the dog? Have you fed the cat?'
I reply, 'Of course I have Mum,
So leave it at that!'
She begins to cook tea but then a disaster!
'Oh no! Oh dear! I've ruined the pasta!'

After dinner, once we've finished our pud,
We have to wash up, just as we should!
'I've spent all evening cooking all this,'
As the tap splutters water, making a hiss,
Once we've finished putting everything away,
We walk into the lounge and on the seats we lay,
Although she can be bossy at times,
She makes funny faces and comedy crimes,
But she's the best ever mum that I could ever get
And I've still got five years to see to her yet!

Robert Anthony John Buckley (13)
Queen Elizabeth's Grammar School, Blackburn

My Family

My family is four plus one
Tall, small, big and strong
But it's the hairy one who is my chum

My family is four plus one
Weird, loving, quarrelsome and sweet
Always my love is curled at my feet

My family is four plus one
Kind, strange, angry and funny
Can you guess who is my best buddy?

My family is four plus one
Mum, Dad, Sister and me
It's the fun we share that sets my heart free

My family is four plus one
Mine forever, together and true
A cold wet nose is your final clue

My family is four plus one
I love with all my heart
And Rosie is the one nestled by the hearth.

Sam Harvey (12)
Queen Elizabeth's Grammar School, Blackburn

My Very Special Family

My family is very strong like me,
My family is actually very sweet,
My family can be a little strict,
My family always act like this,
My family is not always boring,
My family are always helping and trying,
My family are sometimes a little crazy,
My family are even sometimes a little lazy,
My family have many great qualities,
My family are like a big community,
My family are very hard-working,
My family always try their best at everything,
My family are always trying to help me,
My family can be annoying like a buzzing bee,
My family are sometimes in a rush,
My family sometimes stay in a hush,
When I try to think about the facts of my family,
It makes me laugh because I know I have a great family.

Mohammed Tajammel Ismail (12)
Queen Elizabeth's Grammar School, Blackburn

76

My Poem

I started off life on the 9th of May,
Cheerful and busy on my day,
Sadly though I lost my dad,
He moved out and made me feel sad.

However we built our lives back up to an all time high,
Now here I am with my blazer and tie,
Happier than ever and never looking back,
Even though I've had one or two smacks.

My mum is so great,
Always on time and never late,
She helped me talk
And she helped me walk.

My mum is the best,
Better than all the rest,
But best of all,
She isn't too tall.

David Parmenter (13)
Queen Elizabeth's Grammar School, Blackburn

Dreamer

We stuck together like glue,
Did you know I really loved you?

You read to me at night when I always had a fright
Of monsters under my bed
But then you said, 'I love you'
And held me really tight.

I used to think of you as my real dad
Especially when I was ever sad,
I just hope one day I will wake up
And it will have all just been a dream
And you will be standing there with a smile
While holding strawberries and cream.

When they told me, they couldn't control me
But now I know you're looking down on me
And hopefully one day you will see me on the TV.

Sophie Cooper (13)
Queen Elizabeth's Grammar School, Blackburn

Martha And Scott's Reunion

Martha and Scott both missed each other terribly.
They stayed in touch over the Internet.
They couldn't wait to see one another, somewhere, somehow.
So they could reconnect.
Then, Mary took Martha out, so that day came.
Scott was walking down the street as normal.
When there was a voice from behind, calling his name.
As he turned around, he saw those familiar eyes.
Martha.
They both soon realised they hated saying goodbyes
For they meant the end.
The end of a blossoming friendship
A friendship that was reunited by a simple word.
Send.

Charlie Golding (12)
St Bede's RC High School, Ormskirk

78

My Childhood Poem

We wave them off, my brother and I,
From the jetty we depart.
Tossing and turning and bobbing along,
The land getting further and further away!

I'm flying, I'm soaring, nothing can stop us,
Flag flying high like an eagle soaring.
Waves crashing and splashing across our stern,
Excitedly singing the old sea shanties.

But then my eye is drawn elsewhere,
A shapeless steamer breaks through the mist.
Its ominous bow bearing us down,
A whistle primed and ready to blow!

A penetrating blast breaks from my mouth,
Horror sweeps across my frame.
Will it stop, or will it not?
The wait is agony!

But then from out of the mist,
A beacon of hope shines through,
A speedboat breaking the waves, dodging the boats,
A horn is blown, but will it stop?

We sail into the shallow harbour,
To the arms of my mother.
Oh, what a day,
A day to remember!

Alex Aspinwall (12)
St Bede's RC High School, Ormskirk

From My Childhood

Knock, knock on the door
We answered with a smile
In he came and with him he brought
My soulmate in a box

I saw her and gasped
My heart was thumping
The tiniest thing in the world was looking straight at me
I loved her already

Brown and white with that perfect round patch
Her eyes sparkling with curiosity
Her massive personality shining through
She was mine already

She is my star in the dark night
She makes sad times better
She makes me smile when I am down
We play together, making our bond stronger

She's just like me
Active and confident
And maybe too lively for anybody else
That's why she is my dog
My dog, Poppy.

Caitlin Hyland (11)
St Bede's RC High School, Ormskirk

Martha And Scott's Reunion

I bite my nails nervously,
I check the time.
It's 8.58
We're meeting at nine.
My stomach does a flip
As the doorbell rings
I scuffle around
And tidy my things.
I let him in
And we chat for so long
We tell some stories,
We sing a few songs.
We run around and have fun
Just like the old days
He tells loads of jokes
Just like his old ways.
Suddenly it's midnight and he has to go
He'll be back soon of course
I know, I just know.

Caitlin Allt (12)
St Bede's RC High School, Ormskirk

From My Childhood

'Skis parallel!' boomed the French ski instructor.
Mum's response, from under the snow was Anglo Saxon.

The skis flew gracefully off the ramp,
Landing confidently on the crisp, firm ground,
Skilfully weaving through the thin pine trees.
Ted pondered angrily,
Why when he gracefully stepped on his skis,
He went flying down the slopes, going a hundred miles an hour
Knocking and spewing innocent tourists
All over the serene atmosphere of France's finest!

Perhaps this skiing lark isn't for me thought Ted.
Well definitely not for Mum
Because she always lands on her well-bruised bum.
Perhaps one year I will come back to France
With a spring in my step and victory dance.
I'll show that champion skier,
Then he will know he has me to fear!

Ted Thomson (12)
St Bede's RC High School, Ormskirk

From My Childhood

Someone was tapping on my window,
I looked out and saw that someone had been bad,
As God was crying.
Then someone flashed a torch and shot a gun.
I ran to my mum.
Terrified of this person.
But my mum explained that it was just a storm,
Nothing to be afraid of.
So I went back to bed.
But shadows went all along my wall, making funny shapes.
I lay there which made me invisible.
So the shadows went away and the storm finished
And I slipped into another world.

Matilda Walton-Doyle (12)
St Bede's RC High School, Ormskirk

Waiting

It feels like I have been here forever,
just waiting for you to come.
Just stood on this grotty platform,
my heart pounding like a drum.

Every other train seems to have come and gone,
while I have been sat on this bench.
Just typical yours is the very last one,
and with every second I am getting more tense.

That's when I hear it coming,
the rhythm on the track.
I just can't wait for what's coming,
Martha is coming back.

I lurch for the incoming train,
then have to take two steps back.
Because that's when I see your face,
and the memories come flooding back.

Lily Sullivan (12)
St Bede's RC High School, Ormskirk

My Childhood

Boy! You're not the only child in this house now,
My mother has given me a sister.
Boy! Your cat has died,
We found it dead on the lawn.
Boy! You're going to nursery,
I was to go every few days.
Boy! You're going to school,
I'm glad I knew other victims.
Boy! Sometimes I wish you'd grow up,
Who tells me to stop blowing raspberries?
Profound yet ordinary,
Funny yet tragic,
What a different childhood mine was.

Jacob Plumtree (12)
St Bede's RC High School, Ormskirk

83

From My Childhood

Once I was a little girl,
Bright-eyed and not blind.
My first pair of glasses,
Big enough to hide behind.

Once I was a little girl,
The longest hair I'd ever seen.
Chop, chop! Off it popped,
Over to the hairdresser's I had been.

Once I was a little girl,
Lots of friends had I.
When going off to high school,
To a lot of them, I had to say goodbye.

Once I was a little girl,
But now I'm all grown up.
Going out with friends,
Covered in make-up.

Ellie Smith (12)
St Bede's RC High School, Ormskirk

Martha Is Reunited With Scott

Who was that?
I'm sure I've seen him before.
A young, shy looking boy.
I feel so frustrated!
I'm sure I know him.
But where? When?
He was sitting, alone on a table in the park.
Think!
Of course, Scott!
I wonder if he remembers me?
I go over to him, and he says cheerily,
'Hi Martha, I haven't seen you for ages.'

Harry Marston (11)
St Bede's RC High School, Ormskirk

84

Martha And Scott's Reunion

I open my curtains and the sun is shining,
but all I see is grey
don't get me wrong, I love it here
but something is missing
something big, but what?

I walk out the door and there's still something wrong,
I am staring up at the bright blue sky
but the answer is still not there,
I am so confused, my life is perfect
but I am still sad, why?

I just stop and stare and the missing piece is filled,
I see a face, a face I know
I run to him, he runs to me
and for one special moment,
my life is complete
and all the sad memories just disappear.

Annie Bowman (12)
St Bede's RC High School, Ormskirk

From My Childhood

It all started with a click, click, click on the window,
Like a flash I was outside.
Sleek, silver shrapnel fell from the sky,
Like the moon's baby siblings,
An enormous, fat giant gazing at the sky.

There was a bang and a crash,
Man down, man down, I had been hit,
Pure white dust covered me from head to toe.

Glistening in the snow was a silver scrap,
I raced like a bull to pick it up.
It felt cold in the palm of my hand like an ice cube.
My luck was beginning to turn,
It was a two pound coin!

Jake McPherson (12)
St Bede's RC High School, Ormskirk

85

The Ballad Of Martha Dewhurst

I am unhappy,
I just want to cry,
I feel that my whole life is one massive lie,
I wish I was not Martha Dewhurst!

Outside I am weird,
Inside I am sad,
For this I will blame,
My cruel mum and dad,
I wish I was not Martha Dewhurst!

My mean mum and dad,
They make me so sad,
And if I complain,
They bring out the cane,
To hit me with,
Like with my sister,
I wish I was not Martha Dewhurst!

Louisa Gallagher (12)
St Bede's RC High School, Ormskirk

86

Untitled

When I was a child
My behaviour was wild,
It rewarded me a broken arm . . .

I ran around
The playground
With lots of other friends . . .

We fell in a heap,
I began to weep,
Uh oh . . .

It was funny at first
Until my eyes burst,
I could've cried for England . . .

And then the worst came,
My mum did the same,
We fainted at the sight of my x-ray . . .

Harry Murphy (12)
St Bede's RC High School, Ormskirk

A Day From My Childhood

Got up early. Blue kit on. A long journey ahead.
Dad all excited but Mum was really worried.
A huge stadium; bigger than anything I'd ever seen
Millions of people. All in their own colours.
A sea of blue around me.
The other army all in red and white.
The buzz of excitement; the strange chants.
What are they singing?
The players come out. The ref blows his whistle.
The game is underway. I so hope we win.
First one way then the other. They run up the pitch.
Arteta's our hero and he's got the ball.
He shoots. He scores. The crowd go wild.
Dad lifts me up. The noise gets louder.
As Cahill gets the ball. A roar tells me all I need to know.

Everton 2 Sunderland 0.

Steven Meadow (11)
St Bede's RC High School, Ormskirk

Dad's Special Fair Ride!

Dad had put the ladder up,
To fix the broken roof.
Me sitting in the corner,
I watched his every move.
I thought it was a fair ride,
I wanted a go too.
So planned to climb the ladder,
While Dad had gone to the loo.
Clenching onto the sides,
I awkwardly placed my feet,
On the very top of the ladder,
Just for Dad to see.
His face wasn't as I expected,
When he spotted me in mid-air.
Now I suddenly realise,
I am definitely not in a fair.

Alix Riding (12)
St Bede's RC High School, Ormskirk

Love

The brighter the star,
The darker the night,
The fiercer the fighter,
The fiercer the fight,
You want to find treasure,
Well look no more,
The treasure is buried in no gore,
The treasure is buried in the heart,
In the heart where love is found.

Sophie Hannan (11)
St Benedict's Catholic High School, Whitehaven

Cities Of The World

Rome's empire was once, so long
ago Now, a powerful nation.
But in the end it fell,
To commiserations.

Athens was similar,
With its gods and goddesses.
Men wrote the plays
And women wore dresses.

New York is made of dreams
Or so they say.
Inspiring, inviting
Every day.

Paris (pronounced Pa-ree)
Is called the city of romance
But everybody can find themselves
Lost in its dance.

And finally London.
History found in its streets.
Cosmopolitan people
You are waiting to meet.

Eleanor Colquitt (12)
St Benedict's Catholic High School, Whitehaven

Silence

When the world is sad,
Silence saddens me.
When the world is happy,
Silence pleases me.

When evil comes to get me,
Silence soothes me.
When peace seeks me,
Silence cleanses me.

When love fails,
Silence is awkward.
When love is strong,
Silence is beautiful.

When I see my friends,
Silence doesn't follow.
When I see my enemies,
Silence is the key.

When I laugh,
Silence is the enemy.
But when I cry,
Silence is my friend.

Lucy Troughton (14)
St Benedict's Catholic High School, Whitehaven

The Little Bunny

I'm small and furry and I hop around.
I can't jump very high off the ground.
I love my veggies, they're a treat,
I never, ever eat any meat.
With my long ears I hear everything,
Even those stalking foxes, they think they're king.
My nose and whiskers twitch all day long,
We never do anything wrong.

Hannah Pritchard (12)
St Cyres Comprehensive School, Penarth

91

Why?

Fighting a silent battle turns into reality,
This is just the start of a miserable fatality.
Today the death toll is at a mass,
Sounds at a blow that can shatter glass.
One by one the living fall,
The downfall of mankind, the fate of them all.
Madness is breaking every soul in two,
Casting shadows in the pale shade of blue.

The horizon is full of torment and death,
The unknown soldiers save their every last breath.
They are the sea raging through the barren land,
For eternity they will stand.
Like a trail of broken souls they will fight,
For they will be sacrificed for their country tonight.
Bullets are breaking every soul in two,
Casting shadows in the pale shade of blue.

We know nothing of this hell on Earth;
We don't understand what our lives are worth.
Hiding in trenches one moment, then dying the next,
We start to think that our lives aren't perplexed.
While the innocent soldiers fight for their lives,
We are unable to predict who survives.
Gunshots are breaking every soul in two,
Casting shadows in the pale shade of blue.

We go on with our lives while the innocent fall,
While the news and the government forget to tell all.
Story after story, another soldier dies,
How long do we have to listen to these lies?
Equipment failures; far and few,
Are a mean death for one or two.
Again the politicians are breaking every soul in two,
Casting shadows in the pale shade of blue.

How many die? I wish we knew,
It's not only the men, it's the families too.
They've given their lives, one and all,
Nothing so precious as life from our grasp will fall.
This gift is given well and true,
Would this be given if God only knew?
Our faith is breaking every soul in two,
Casting shadows in the pale shade of blue.

The futility of war is there for all to see,
It shows what a waste people's lives can be.
As their lives are on the brink,
Three score and ten is what we think.
An eye for an eye, a tooth for a tooth,
Not making twenty, that's the painful truth.
Guns, bombs and people are breaking every soul in two,
Coffins draped in red, white and blue.

Clair Roberts (15)
St Cyres Comprehensive School, Penarth

Where Do I Belong?

Where do I fit in in the world?
Is there a point to me?
Should I just be invisible,
Or shall I just simply be me?
I feel excluded from the rest,
I know I'm different to the best.
Is there a place where I belong?
Maybe I could stay there for quite long.
If I was where I felt at home,
I would love it, even if I was stuck in my own little dome.
When I wake up in the morning
I think to myself,
If I wasn't myself
I would be boring!
So I am proud to be me.

Amy Morgan (12)
St Cyres Comprehensive School, Penarth

When I Was A Girl

'When I was a girl,'
My mother would say,
'We never used to
Get our own way!

We'd follow the rules,
Do things by the book!
We'd all take our turns
To clean and to cook!

Our tops weren't low cut,
Our skirts to our knees!
We always said, 'Thank you',
We always said, 'Please.'

I was always a good girl
And never a brat!
Oh, darling daughter,
Why can't you be like that?'

'Well, Mother, it's hard
To be good day and night.
Never to argue
And never to fight!

To always be brilliant,
To always be good.
Believe me, Mother,
I would if I could!

I'll never be perfect,
So don't get me stressed,
Just believe me, dear Mother,
I do try my best!'

Laura Clarke (14)
St Cyres Comprehensive School, Penarth

Helpless

Children out there are getting abused.
You may think they eat, but they don't.
Starvation isn't a problem with them anymore;
It's the deep cuts that run for miles.
They are all over their bodies,
So deep they never end.

Love doesn't touch their heart,
It's like paper torn into millions of pieces.
Their habitat is in the dark; a cold cave.
Their parents say they are home-schooling them,
But the only education they're getting is abuse.

Nobody knows what they are holding back.
They have the bruises that will scar them for life.
Neighbours wonder but don't ask.
It's hard to see behind their mess.

When we hear them crying at night,
We turn our backs and go back to sleep.
And then the next morning it'll be too late,
But they'll be up there where they are loved.

Sara Gamil Rahman (15)
St Cyres Comprehensive School, Penarth

My Life

I woke up in the morning and I brushed my hair,
I went down for breakfast and instead I had a pear.
I asked my mum, 'Can I have a banana?'
I went outside and met my friend, Rhianna.
I went on my bike and I went to school,
We went on a school trip and it was so cool.
We got off the bus, it was time to go home,
I had my tea and an ice cream cone!

Nadine Ismail (11)
St Cyres Comprehensive School, Penarth

The Lovely Daffodil

The lovely daffodil lives vividly in the sun
Bright petals reflect the morning dewdrops
She sings to thank the sun for her refreshing light.

The lovely daffodil grows elegantly in the drizzles of rain
Her enchanting scent increased by the hour!
Her flexibility is rare but tries to look fit.

The lovely daffodil dances in the elegant wind
She has beautiful flowing locks
Golden as the sun above!

The lovely daffodils gracefully waltzing
With their soulmate partners
Aaaahhhh!

The lovely daffodil pivots from side to side
Laughing, chatting, prancing and dancing
Twirling and twirling until dizzy!

The lovely daffodil lives
Until
Next year!

Ruth Miser (15)
St Cyres Comprehensive School, Penarth

Hamster

H armless
A dorable
M ass multipliers
S tupid
T ime wasters
E xpensive
R eal cute.

Connor Singleton (12)
St Cyres Comprehensive School, Penarth

Steadfast

Something to lean on
When everything falls,
Someone to ask for,
Someone to call,
Someone to sit when
You're too weak to stand,
Someone to hold you,
A lifeline, a hand,
My legs, if you need them,
When yours have grown numb,
A brain when the pain
Has stricken yours dumb,
A heart when a heart
Is all that you need
And eyes with some tears left
And lungs that can breathe,
A light in the darkness
Where nothing else shines
And if you need a shoulder to cry on,
Use mine.

Amy Sleeman (15)
St Cyres Comprehensive School, Penarth

97

Sport!

S occer
P olo
O lympics
R ugby
T ennis

S ports
P eople
O ften
R ewarded for
T alent

A nd are
N ever
D isappointing

S occer
P olo
O lympics
R ugby
T ennis.

Luke Garland (12)
St Cyres Comprehensive School, Penarth

The Cat And The Rabbit

The cat and the rabbit having fun
They had tea and buns
The cat had two kittens, the rabbit had two sons,
The cat and the rabbit went for a run.
They fell down a hill and bumped their bums.
They were getting hungry and rubbed their tums,
So they met a mouse
Who took them back to his house.
The cat and the rabbit went up the hill to get a pail of milk,
The cat and the rabbit drank the milk
And it made their fur as smooth as silk.

Georgina Mitchell (12)
St Cyres Comprehensive School, Penarth

My Remedy Reverie

I look around me, there are people everywhere.
Tall people, small people, a flash of golden hair.
So many, so different, walking side by side,
Yet so oblivious to me watching them as they pass on by.

I watch these different people in their own little worlds.
It's interesting to watch them, see their characters unfurl.
Some of them are on a mission, passing to and fro,
Walking fast, never looking back, always on the go.

There's others that look lonely, others that look sad.
Others are with their family, or just out with the lads.
Some of them stare back at me, their piercing glares cut deep,
They look at me like I'm an animal; a homeless beggar
on the streets.

No one seems to care when they see my dirty clothes,
They walk away, without a second glance, looking down their nose.
Finally, the sun starts to set; I am pulled out of my remedy reverie
And I remember where I am, I remember the failure that is me.

Ellen Mahenthiralingam (13)
St Cyres Comprehensive School, Penarth

What Makes A Friend?

It's something warm,
It's something sweet,
But it is not something that you eat.
It makes you happy but sometimes sad,
It's a feeling almost everyone has.
It's something that's quite hard to explain,
It's like a list of feelings and pain.
I'm not going to tell you what it is yet,
I'm afraid, my friend, you'll just have to guess.
They listen to your troubles,
They can help you out,
You may have arguments and start to shout,
But half of the times you patch over
The things you did rough.
OK, OK, I think I'll give in.
I'm going to say that it is a friend.
So pass the penny and don't let it end.

Seren Cain (12)
St Cyres Comprehensive School, Penarth

Wondering?

Does every cloud have a silver lining?
Does every rainbow have a pot of gold?
Does every parting have such sweet sorrow?
Is every story a tale to be told?

Is every joy a joy to be shared?
Is every bridge meant to be crossed?
Is every day a new tomorrow?
Does every win mean something is lost?

Why is a song a song worth singing?
Why does every dream have a chance to come true?
Why is every friend a friend worth knowing?
Really? Is this all true?

Sam Rayer (14)
St Cyres Comprehensive School, Penarth

1o0

The Shoes

These are the shoes
That she trudged about in
Wandering around the swishing woods
Going walking with her dog, Charlie
The flowers dancing in the wind

These are the shoes
That she took to Dunolly
Walking near the glinting gorge
River-rafting, freezing cold
Climbing up the wall
Finally she reached the top

But these are not the shoes
That she goes to school in
Going from class to class
Watching TV
After her homework

These are not the shoes
That she plays hockey in
Passing the ball
Catching the ball
The goalkeeper looking like a Transformer
On the pitch

But these are the shoes
That she keeps in the cupboard
Waiting for her next adventure.

Katica Jacobs (11)
St Margaret's School, Edinburgh

They Lie

I remember waiting for you behind
the dusty brick wall behind the garden
beneath the autumn sun and withering leaves

Careful of the thorns and nettles!
But we weren't bothered about those things
you said nothing could conquer love

Your black hair and thick glasses
hid some lost secrets not even I
could seek or comprehend

I remember finding you, deep cuts
deep cuts in each arm. Warbling the whippoorwill.
Begging the heavens to pardon you

Your face in a flush, you
softly spoke of those past times
when the cards were dealt the right way

And so I apologise for giving you false hope
beneath those harvest moons behind the
famous wall that kept our memories in

Do not be fooled by those that tell you
love conquers all.
They lie.

Arusa Qureshi (17)
St Margaret's School, Edinburgh

102

The Shoes

These are the shoes
That went to Australia and back,
When they walked on the hard, dusty road
And saw kangaroos and koalas
When they played on the haystacks
And in the garden with a bat and ball
These are the shoes
That walked on the warm, sandy beach
When she licked her cold ice cream

These are not the shoes
That went to the zoo and saw animals swing and jump
These are not the shoes
That she does her homework in
When she is tired and worried
These are not the shoes
That go to school when she writes and thinks
Trying to work out what to say
This is because she has grown older
And no longer needs them
But she remembers those carefree shoes with a smile.

Phoebe Haddon (11)
St Margaret's School, Edinburgh

Her Boots

These are the boots
That she ran wild in,
That she clambered up onto the big black horse in,
That softly hit the ground
When the fun was over.
These are the boots
That she played 'make-believe' in,
That she twirled around and around and around in
On that sunny Sunday afternoon.
These are the boots that were paraded down the sand in,
Which would come home loved and torn.

These are no longer the boots
That she glides gracefully down the slopes in,
And they're not the boots she wears striding down the high street.
But sometimes, just sometimes,
She takes them out to relive her happy childhood memories . . .
Just for a while.

Anna Hawkes-Cumming (11)
St Margaret's School, Edinburgh

Why Is This, I Wonder?

Lights and candles flicker above,
Showing something like a dove,
Beautiful, but surely sinister,
Why is this, I wonder?

Tempers boil and news is spread
Of stars flying, whilst in our beds.
Blood is given and is shed,
Why is this, I wonder?

Arms are risen and music played,
Children cry in the shade,
Suddenly a man does fall,
Why is this, I wonder?

Tears drip from wet eyes,
Yet mine drip in gladness.
I am wrong, I am right,
Why is this, I wonder?

Koren Murphy (13)
St Margaret's School, Edinburgh

Within

Within the cold there burns a fire,
Within the fire there burns the wood,
Within the wood there burns a story.

And in the story there are words,
And in the words there is meaning,
And in the meaning there is history.

Within the history lies a secret,
Within the secret there waits a lie,
Within the lie there burns a sadness.

And in the sadness there lies a cause,
And in the cause there lies a cure,
But in the cure there waits a sacrifice.

Within the sacrifice there lies a hope,
Within the hope there burns a flame,
Within the flame the cold has ceased.

Beth Clarke (14)
St Margaret's School, Edinburgh

106

Spring

Spring flowers
Over the dew-kissed meadows
Joining the birds
And watching them fly
Spreading colour from her heart
Giving joy from the midnight sky

Spring glows
In warming pastures
When she sings
It's like a melody to the ear
With diminuendos
And crescendos
The world is bright
When she is near.

Anna Cullinan (11)
St Margaret's School, Edinburgh

War

Throngs of men were lined up like helpless robots
ready to charge on command.
Left, right, left, right, left, right, it began.
Sweat leaked from every part of my body;
my eyes wept due to the rotting aroma of inhumanity
that pricked and prodded every time I took a dark step.
My heartbeat increased immensely.
My heart almost burst out of my chest, and my legs gave way
and almost plunged my tattered body to the grubby ground.
Trudging along, I was skimming bullets by the minute;
I could feel it crawling up me.
Silently I sobbed, I could feel it pulsing and
throbbing through my veins like a train making
its way to a specific destination.
I could feel it eating, devouring and consuming
every part of me . . . fear.
Its taste was poisonous, a deadly taste of fear.
It ripped open my heart.
'Take cover, men!' I heard the sergeant holler.
'Move, men, move! Put your masks on!'
Swiftly, men weaved, ducked and tried in vain
to escape from the gas that was ominously stalking
its brand new prey.
If you could see hate, gas is what it would look like.
The sirens yelled out to the soldiers the all clear.
Everyone was uplifted with relief.
It was short lived.
'Look,' someone suddenly screamed, 'a bomb!'
No one could move, we were frozen with fear.
There was nothing we could do. We were . . . trapped!
I roared with fear!
Bang. Black. Smoke. It was all over!
Thousands where dead.

Kirsty Wheelhouse (13)
St Mary's RC High School, Blackpool

108

Why I Ran

This is me,
But you don't see me for who I am.
So this is my story,
Why I ran
Back in my home.
Where fire breaks the skies
And a red sea fills us with sorrow,
Bodies lie in an eternal rest,
And although we aren't acquainted,
It still darkens our hearts with guilt.
We're not so different,
So why did it start?
Why can't it end?
These questions scare my mind,
The cold spear of death.
It grew closer to me
So I ran!
Through the war of Hell
And Satan's pit.
But now I dream
How can it be,
Here in a heavenly place?
So next time think,
When you're in bed,
Think of me
And being there,
So then you will know
Why I ran!

Mathew Boddy (14)
Sandhill View School, Sunderland

Child Labour

I walk down the street
After slaving away in the mines.
We are all starving for something to eat,
And I am as dirty as a bin.
I am a victim of child labour.

It's the year 1880 and Victoria rules.
I work all day - in the dark.
Low wages and long hours,
I'm really fed up with this lark.
I'm a victim of child labour.

I'm only eight years old,
And I'm lucky to be alive.
I shiver in the cold,
As nobody cares for us.
I'm a victim of child labour.

Many people die in the mines,
It's the thing I worry about most.
Explosions, fires, deaths everywhere,
I can only pray that the next day I'm not a ghost.
I'm a victim of child labour.

Children shouldn't be treated this way,
We are all forced into this,
We have no say,
As I'm keeping my family alive.
I'm a victim of child labour.

Nathan Davison (13)
Sandhill View School, Sunderland

I Wish

I wish I had everything,
I wish I had it all,
I wish I had money,
I wish I could have more.

I wish I had books,
I wish I had good looks,
I wish I had dogs,
I wish I had clogs,
I wish and I wish.

But I never get anything,
It just isn't fair,
I mean, come on,
Is it too much to ask?

I wish I had cars,
I wish I had chocolate bars,
I wish I had flippers,
I wish I had slippers,
I wish, I just wish.

But I never get anything,
Anything at all.
My mam tells me to wait,
But really, just really,
Do I ask for much?

Adam Huskinson (12)
Sandhill View School, Sunderland

BFL

'Please, Miss Johnson, don't give me a C3.
I promise to be good so don't hate me.'

'Fine, fine, you have one more chance.
Only if you get up and do a dance.'

'OK, OK, but I don't want one.'
'Well come on then, dance.'
'OK, I will dance. Is it OK if I prance?

Please Miss, please Miss, don't give me a C3.'
'I know, but you've been naughty.'
'I know, but it's just me.'

'Please Miss, no C3.'
'Why? Why?'
'Because as I say, it's just me.'
'Well I suppose I'll let you off

But . . .
You've had enough chances in my class.'
'I know, but I won't . . .'
'Shut up, C3! Get out, or do you want a C4?'

Aiden Davison (12)
Sandhill View School, Sunderland

Please, Mam

'Please, Mam, please
Can I go out
With my friends
And then shout?'

'Yes, my dear,
You shall now go,
As long as you don't throw
Rocks or stones or anything sharp,
Or I will bark!'

Tyler-Jo Wright (12)
Sandhill View School, Sunderland

Morbid Love

I'm afraid I'll have to tell you
That my heart is broken inside,
Because now I live without you,
To your love I can't abide.
I write this in thought of you,
To remind you of my love,
The times we shared together,
Have now flown away like doves.
I'm really lost without you,
And I can't do this anymore.
I'm afraid of this one word, but
It's time to close the door.

So I guess this is goodbye, au revoir, farewell,
Because now the bag is tying round my head
So let's not dwell.
But basically what I'm trying to do
By writing these few words,
Is tell, my beloved,
That I'll always love you.

Niall Massingham (12)
Sandhill View School, Sunderland

I Really, Really Miss You!

I wish I could see you, Mummy, in Heaven above,
I'm the only person that loves you the most.

Earth was her Hell,
Heaven was her dream,
That's how long it has been.

Love you, miss you lots,
I still get belly knots.
You are the thunder and I am the lightning.

Sophie Holyoak (14)
Sandhill View School, Sunderland

113

Doing Detention

'Miss, Miss,
Will you tell me
Why I got a big C3?'

'Jordon, Jordon,
You started bugging me
When you swilled Lee
With a can of Pepsi.'

'But Jan, Jan,
That doesn't explain why I got a C3.
It just keeps on getting to me.

I never meant to spill the can on the fan,
Or hit the man or steal the van,
So I just ran.'

'Well I never knew about any of that,
When you kicked the cat or called someone fat.'

'OK, OK, I might as well do the detention
but remember this, I will always pay attention!'

Jordon Dryden (12)
Sandhill View School, Sunderland

I Support Sunderland

Sunderland's the team I support,
They weren't very good, I always thought,
But after that I changed my mind,
We got Steve Bruce and then we 'shined'.

Sunderland play in red and white,
They also play at the Stadium of Light.
We played Newcastle and beat them too,
I support Sunderland and so should you.

Bradley Barraclough (13)
Sandhill View School, Sunderland

114

Is It Cream, Grey Or White?

Is it cream, grey or white?
All we know is that it's bright.
Is it death or is it life?
All we know is it comes out at night

Is it yellow, orange or red?
All we know is that it gets you out of bed.
Is it hot or is it cold?
All we know is it glistens like gold.

Is it dark or is it light?
All we know is that it's at a height.
Is it dry or is it wet?
All we know is it goes down with the sunset.

Is it cream, grey or white?
All we know is that it's bright.
Is it death or is it life?
All we know is it comes out at night.

Alix Blissett (12)
Sandhill View School, Sunderland

The Black Cats

T he stadium of light
H owls at night
E very day

B ut the footballers are ready for the pay
L ovely day out
A ll the crowd just shout
C 'mon
K ilmarnock we are playing

C heat, cheat, it's all they do
A lmost time to go
T ick-tock, it's time to go
S underland put on a great show.

Andrew Dodsworth (13)
Sandhill View School, Sunderland

115

British Culture

The idea of tea
It sounds good to me
Go down the pub
To get some lovely grub

God save the Queen
Support my favourite team
From riding the London bus
To the top of Loch Lomond, Luss

Reading William Shakespeare
Living on the Wear
It's almost always overcast
And the summer sun doesn't last

From the Prime Minister's Number 10
To the great Christopher Wren
To America, our great mates
All of these make Britain great!

Curtis Taylor (14)
Sandhill View School, Sunderland

If That Was Me

Would you be like that,
If that was me
Lying beneath the cliff,
Lifeless?

Would you care
If that was me
Hanging from the ceiling,
My eyes empty?

Would you shed a tear
If that was me
In a pool of crimson blood,
Wishing you were here with me?

Kate Williamson (12)
Sandhill View School, Sunderland

116

Heartbroken

When a heart is broken
There is no replacement.
I miss you more each minute.
I promise you, at this moment,
I regret what I did.
But now you are inaccessible,
My heart is torn to shreds,
There's nothing that can fix it,
I might as well be dead.
I don't get much sleep at night,
I can't eat or drink,
I love you more each second,
You're all my mind can think.
But now you have forgotten me,
I'll be on my way.
I forgot to tell you,
I miss you more each day.

Caitlin Craword (13)
Sandhill View School, Sunderland

Love

I think about you all the time,
I bet I don't cross your mind.
Keep you apart, so deep in my heart,
Separate you from the rest
Because I like you the very best.
We are two souls with one thought,
What is love but a lion roaring in our hearts?

The thought is love which we have a lot of,
Our love is like a star, it will be there for evermore.
You and me are meant to be,
Like the moon shining gently.
What is love but a lion roaring in our hearts?

Megan Phillips (13)
Sandhill View School, Sunderland

117

Sorry

Sorry, sorry,
I'm so sorry
For whatever I've done.

Ouch, ouch,
Daddy, that hurts,
Please stop hitting me.

There's no one around
And look what I've found,
Blood all over my face.

I feel so sad
Because of what I've just had,
A huge, big punch in the face.

As I fall to the floor
My eyes start to close,
I still love you, Daddy.

Charlotte Carter (13)
Sandhill View School, Sunderland

Heaven

I wish Heaven had a phone
So I could hear your voice again.
I thought of you today,
But that's nothing new.
I thought about you yesterday,
And days before that too.
All I have left is memories
And a picture in a frame.
Your memory is a keepsake
Which will never part . . .
God has you in his arms
And I have you in my heart.

Cecilia Davison (13)
Sandhill View School, Sunderland

118

Fred

I had a pet snail,
Small, slimy and hard as a nail.
He used to slime all over my bed
And his name was Fred.
My mam didn't like him very much,
She wouldn't even give him the slightest touch.
Until I taught him how to swim
And kept him fit in the gym.
He started to get very fast,
Everything was a huge blast.
Papers wanted pictures . . .
Flash
Smash
Trash

Fred is dead!

Jessica Cowling (13)
Sandhill View School, Sunderland

Eternal Darkness

Darkness shadows the empty night
To keep its creatures out of sight.
The mother's sun has gone to bed,
Only to rest its sleepy head.
The moonlight coils around the trees,
The dark infects like a disease.
Owls - they hoot, wolves - they howl,
At the midnight's evil scowl.
The beast will die when light is shone,
At dawn the darkness will be gone.
Say goodbye to dark of night,
Hello to eternal rays of light.

Jarit Roffe (13)
Sandhill View School, Sunderland

Wind

The wind blows hard, the wind blows soft,
The wind, a quick breeze or just short,
The wind blows the leaves of autumn,
The wind flows like lava and the people like the shelter,
The wind brings the heat,
The wind brings the calm,
The wind is just the wind.

Andrew Pringle (13)
Sandhill View School, Sunderland

The Lightning

Flick'ring through the sky it crackles,
Lighting up the woods.
Flying through the clouds
Leaving thunder in its wake.
It pauses in the darkness as it looks at the world below.
In the darkness it starts to glow.
It snickers as it plots,
The forest below would soon begin to shine.
It jumped from the cloud and
As it flickered and burned
The following thunder gave a word of woe.
It struck the wood and began to glow.
The crows took flight as the fire took hold.
The lightning snickered as its work was done,
Until tomorrow when it would burn again.

Joshua Nixon (12)
Slemish College, Ballymena

Cherry Blossoms

Cherry blossoms on the tree
Remind me of a memory
Of scattered pink petals everywhere
And my heart shining like the sun.

The warmth disappeared and the bitter winds
Swept through like a silent storm,
Breaking all that I held dear
And leaving me alone.

Desperately I clawed and cried
To cling to my old life.
Through the winter my heart bled for you
And your words cut like a knife.

Each time I think I can let go
And move along the road
Another thought
Another dream
Drags me back to September again.

My memories come back again
They tell me you're all wrong
But when did I care about that before?
And these days I'm messed up too.

It's spring again, I've made it through
But my heart can't be quite whole
The summer will come
And I'm still me
But you took everything that I owned.

Jordanne Clarke (15)
Slemish College, Ballymena

Colours

You look at me from front to back
But still can't see my colours.
You look at me up and down
But still can't see my colours.
You look at me from side to side
But still can't see my colours.
You tap me on the shoulder.
I turn and you say, 'Hey.'
We talk a while
And then you smile.
You must have found my colours.

Caoimhe Moreland (15)
Slemish College, Ballymena

I Am Who I Am

So what, I'm not like you!
So what, just because I don't smoke
What does it make me?
So what, I'm good in school, maybe
I want to be.
So what, teachers may like me
But only for being good.
So what, I don't fight, maybe
I don't want to hurt people.
So what, I think before I say something,
That's because I don't want to hurt anyone.
So what, I'm quiet, doesn't mean
I don't say things that are true!
I am who I am
If you don't like me that's your problem
Like me or hate me, I don't care
I am who I am, this is who I will always be
Just accept me for who I am
I am who I am.

Sophie Lauren Kyle (12)
The Elton High School, Bury

122

I Am Who I Am

Just because I have a tag
And just because I'm bad
Doesn't mean I'm never glad
Just because you have an issue
Doesn't mean I'll hunt you down and kill you
I am who I am
You see people on the streets
Stamping their feet to the beats
Just because I drink alcohol
Doesn't mean I'm the person you don't want to know
Just because I smoke
Doesn't mean I do coke
I am who I am
Don't judge me because I'm a G
I want respect with lots of company
Just because I wear a hoodie
Doesn't mean I'm not funny
Just because you think I'm mad
Doesn't mean I take after my dad
I am who I am and I am glad
So next time you see a chav
Doesn't mean you should think he's sad
You don't even know the guy
Just give him a rest
And a bit of time
So I am who I am
And don't judge me for what I'm not.

Callum Brady (12)
The Elton High School, Bury

How I Feel At 14

I'm angry at the world,
I feel I don't fit in.
This life is like a race,
Though I will never win.
I've tried all those things,
I thought would make me cool,
But I still hate my life,
And dickheads at school.

All of my anger builds deep inside,
What to do, I must decide.
How to use it, I do not know,
It's always in me, wherever I go.
In one big lot, it will always come out,
Bang, punch, snap or one big shout.
Like a volcano I want to erupt,
A boom, an explosion, my anger's overtook.

Everyone is better,
And I will not succeed.
Everyone's a plant,
And I am still a seed.
Everyone's a person,
And I am just a figure.
Everyone's a story,
But I'm a black and white picture.

Marcus Close (14)
The Elton High School, Bury

124

The Idea Media

Much too much TV spewing out hate,
Much too much focus on crime and rape,
Much too much negativity on the young generation,
Nor enough joy across our once great nation,
Much too much bad news being repeated,
Much too many British being conceited.

Now for a change let's be quiet and humble
And let the rest of the world moan and grumble,
We need to take the focus off the credit crunch
Focus on Obama's and Cameron's White House brunch,
We need to take each other by the hand
And make sure we sort out our once great land.

We need to get behind the South African dream,
The World Cup comes back with our English team,
This will start the slow speed prospect of getting our nation back on its feet,
Our hopes and dreams and what we live for bow down to eleven Englishmen's feet.

Let's stand together in our separate groups,
The moshers, the chavs and our great, great troops.

Let's bring our nation back to glory,
To complete this chapter and start anew in this never-ending story!

Liam Greer (14)
The Elton High School, Bury

Just Because

Just because I don't do stupid things,
     does that make me a loser?
Just because I like school,
     does that make me a swot?
Just because I dress differently,
     does that make me stupid?
Just because I'm a different colour,
     does that make me different?

Am I a loser because
     I'm smart?
Am I ugly because
     I'm not Cheryl Cole?
Am I horrible because
     I'm not rich?

Black, white, rich, poor, skirts, shorts,
Smart, stupid, ugly, pretty, good, bad.

I'm normal
I do the same things as you
     Can do
The same things as you.

But I won't be the
     Same as you.

Eloise Pierce (12)
The Elton High School, Bury

126

Friendship

True friendship is unbreakable,
There are blips of hatred along the way,
Enemies try to tear it apart,
But you let your friendship stay.

Our paths may be different,
But our friendship is strong,
We have the same interests,
Thus, our friendship will be long.

I'm proud to be your friend,
I will support your decisions,
However, I will not let you do wrong,
As I cherish our friendship, whilst it is strong.

Our friendship is a castle,
It is difficult to infiltrate,
It takes a great force to penetrate,
I will fight the battle.

When the battle is won,
Our friendship will stun,
Like the sight of the sun,
The deed will be done . . .

Jacob Dean (14)
The Elton High School, Bury

Racism

Black people are disrespected,
They would like it if they were respected.
Why does colour, skin, country define us?
Why do we think that
They don't share the same qualities?
Why can we not be brothers and sisters
And friends and family and neighbours?
Why are some people so racist?
They are no different to us.

Joseph Bradshaw (13)
The Elton High School, Bury

127

Goal Number 4!

I'm only a fullback,
Looking for a goal,
And when it came
I hit the post -
Lucky for me
It rebounded home.

I put on my shin pads,
I put on my boots.
I was feeling nervous
As we warmed ourselves up.

The first half was drawing to a close
As I thought there was no goal -
But then the moment came.

I'm only a fullback,
Looking for a goal,
And when it came
I hit the post -
Lucky for me
It rebounded home.

Liam Horrobin (14)
The Elton High School, Bury

Words

Words, they pierce directly to the heart
Words, they're as sticky as a tart
Words, they smash and crush
Words, they hold tons on us
Words, they don't say much
Words, they don't need to touch
Words, they make you kneel
Words; you can't punch through steel.
This is my message of the day
Please; think before you say!

Liam Salwa (12)
The Elton High School, Bury

128

Don't Put Me Down

Are you saying this to me in this cold dark room?
While I wait for your answer up on the stage,
Lights beam down on me as you judge me,
The audience are waiting, can't you see?
Then, my judge opens their mouth,
'You can't be in a band because you don't look like Cheryl Cole,
When you sing, give it more soul,
You're not good at maths so not a teacher.'
This judge is a monstrous creature,
'You're not tall enough to be a model even with make-up done, hair curled,
You don't like planes, so why travel the world?
You've never watched the Olympics, you'd never get gold,
You're so childish, in the future you'd never have your own child to hold.
You can't be famous because you're petrified of cameras.
That dream of working with dolphins, lions, tigers and pandas,'
As I watch this judge laugh I realise who it is,
It's funny what your mind can think,
You're the put down, the judge, actor, or clown.

Elle Finch (12)
The Elton High School, Bury

Eminem

Eminem, what a guy,
His music is amazing, I hope he doesn't die.
He is an amazing rapper,
He is a real yapper.
Crack a bottle, toy soldiers,
Keeps his lyrics in folders.
He is wicked as you can hear,
His favourite animal is definitely deer.
And his best drink is beer,
He drives his Porsche in second gear.

Blake Richards (13)
The Elton High School, Bury

129

Tests

Stressed because of the test.
Tests are difficult,
I hate tests,
A bad game, I will be sad.

Mum and Dad will go mad.
SATs should be sacked.
Horror to the eye,
Terror can be applied.

Silence in the room.
It will be over soon.
Not to worry,
No need to hurry.

Done and dusted,
Just in time.
I feel better now,
It may be over,
But that is just the start.

Josh Molyneux (12)
The Elton High School, Bury

Miseducation

Life is unfair,
Life is too short,
These are the phrases that people say
But they are the ones whose lives are grey,
Dull and misery spread far and vast,
Just killing the dreams of people to come.
The politicians are no more,
Horrors to the eye, the drugs and violence.

Why don't people just turn around
And see the good of the world?
The teachers, the schools, the place of learning
Are where dreams come true.

Umayr Ali (11)
The Elton High School, Bury

My Loved Heart Rabbit

Air so cold
Heat not near
How am I
Such a gleam?

Covers so clean
Food so near
Water makes me
Such a dream.

Dreams so clear
Owners so loved
Love so warm
My heart so touched.

And then all at once
It all blew away
All my love around me
Just all blew around me
And flew straight away.

Stephanie Hill (13)
The Elton High School, Bury

Life

Life is a misunderstood thing.
People live and people die.
Some people just can't bear life.
Some people just embrace life.
Life is taken by war.
The men that lie dead
Get engulfed by death.

As time goes by everybody dies.
The clock counts down every second.
With this nobody wants to die.
Birth and death,
This is the cycle of life.

Kieran Ashworth (12)
The Elton High School, Bury

131

This Generation

This generation, oh this generation
This generation I was born
At the age of four I went to school
I even learnt to swim in the pool
At the age of eight I made a bezzy mate
I got a good result in my test
It doesn't mean I'm not cool
I am no fool
This generation, oh this generation
This generation I was born
Crime stealing and killing, when will all this end?
Why not notice this new trend?
Just cos I'm not involved in these acts
It doesn't mean I'm quiet - that's a fact
This generation, oh this generation
This generation I was born
I am who I am and I always will be
I don't care what you say, no one can change me!

Aishah Saddiqa (12)
The Elton High School, Bury

My Family

I love my family
No one can stop me
Although . . .

My name is Leah
My dad likes beer
My mum likes to shop
My sister likes to shout
My sister likes me
I love my dog called Scooby
People might say I'm weird but I put up with it
But still no one can stop me loving them
Even if they don't love me.

Leah Myers (11)
The Elton High School, Bury

132

Eternal Warrior

He went to battle, with few by his side,
He tried to stop them, but they defied,
They wouldn't listen, the ignorant foes,
Lined up in thousands of columns and rows
They were ready to fight, ready to kill him,
His chances of survival were indeed very slim,
Though he fought like a lion, he was heavily outnumbered,
'Kill him!' the enemies thundered,
Swords and spears soared through the air,
One on one? They wouldn't dare,
Because he was so very strong,
They didn't want to wait very long,
He fell to the earth, with arrows in his chest,
Knowing that he had done his best,
But they didn't care, but they didn't see,
That they had wronged for eternity,
Should they have killed him? They weren't sure,
But an eternal warrior he will be for evermore.

Mohammad Zain Hassan (14)
The Elton High School, Bury

About Me And My Mates

I support Man Utd,
Liverpool is hated,
I love Abi,
My cat is very tabby.
My mate is called Nathan,
Josh is hated,
My mate Nathan will go out with Olivia on a later date,
It's a true love made with fate.
My hobbies include tree climbing
And there is a search engine called Bing,
I play football,
But I hate to fall.

Bradley Smith (12)
The Elton High School, Bury

133

Chances

England's like the ying and yang with terrorists and gangs,
With cars getting blown to bits, no wonder people ain't fans.
We read in the papers and hear on the air
Of crime, stealing and killing everywhere.
They blame the children, they lead us astray,
We find opportunities but they say go away.
They tell us we're to blame for all the world's troubles (yeah right),
Sorry to burst your bubble but England's not like the ying and yang,
Too much evil in horrible gangs.
There's not enough love, no sign of doves
Because we're not the ones who make the drugs
Or climb the highest mountain
Just to say horrible words like a polluted fountain.
If they gave us a chance we would be fine
Instead of sitting and wasting our time.
We are the future and not the past,
Our time is coming really fast.

Tonderai Utsiwegota (12)
The Elton High School, Bury

Rainbow!

Look at you with the pretty pattern
I love that colour blue
When I look at you everything feels so true.

And look at that colour pink,
You always put a twinkle in my eye
Every time I look at you so high in the sky.

And look at the colour green
It is just like something I have never seen
I love that colour
It looks like I could erase you with a rubber.

Oh little rainbow you are so amazing
You have now got everybody gazing.

Sinead Tiltman (13)
The Elton High School, Bury

134

The First Day Of School

There I was putting my tie on
As the glowing, bright sun shone,
I walked downstairs with a smile on my face
As I struggled to tie my shoelace,
I stepped outside with a cheesy grin,
But sadly I banged my shin,
I stumbled across a 10 foot tree,
With a buzzing bumblebee!
I ran away as fast as I could,
As my feet were going *thud, thud, thud!*
I finally arrived at Elton High,
Some people in Year 11 were as high as the sky.
My friends called me over
As they tapped me on the shoulder.
This was my first day of Elton High,
Even though I was a little bit shy!

Luan Barber-Norton (12)
The Elton High School, Bury

I'll Treat You The Same

Our minds may be different,
I'll treat you the same,
You may be different,
I'll treat you the same,
You may have an illness,
I'll treat you the same,
You may have a different accent,
I'll treat you the same,
You're from a different social class,
I'll treat you the same,
You may be a different size,
I'll treat you the same,
You be nice to me,
I'll treat you the same.

Curtis Ryan McCann (14)
The Elton High School, Bury

135

My Sister

She is funny, kind and she is smart too,
but being annoying, is what she likes to do.
She loves to play tig, and play on the slide,
it's safe to say, she likes the outside.
Her favourite film is 'Tinkerbell',
it's about a fairy, who fell down a well.
She loves to draw, colour and paint,
my mother says, that she is a saint.
She's always watching, something on the TV,
her favourite programme is CBeebies.
She loves Christmas, 'cause she gets lots of toys,
she says, 'Ha ha, I've got more than the boys!'
Her favourite sport, is of course football,
she can't be the keeper because she's too small.
And last of all,
I love my sister!

Daniel Trundle (14)
The Elton High School, Bury

Sports

Football shirts and cricket bats,
Tennis balls and those silly baseball hats.
Fans, supporters screaming out loud,
The ball goes up and into the crowd.
Running and jumping, heading and hitting,
But for people who don't like sports let's stick to boring old knitting.
When I'm there the stadium's buzzing,
But when it's finished, all that shoving.
The final score that's three points for us,
Now we come back on the bus.
We get home, have our tea,
Patrice Evra's number is number three.
Later on we watch 'Sky Sports' and 'Match of the Day',
Well done boys, football's worth the pay.

Joe Mulhall (12)
The Elton High School, Bury

New Beginnings

I look up to see the tears falling,
The new beginning is calling,
Calling my name,
It's great but such a shame.

I miss my best friend,
I thought our friendship would never end,
But it's time to start again,
Inside my heart feels slight pain,
But I look up to see my friends smiling back at me,
Like we were always meant to be.

So I am afraid to say,
It is my last day,
But the memories of primary
Will appear to last forever,
Forever in my heart!

Charlotte Emily Gillespie (12)
The Elton High School, Bury

Football Mad!

As you can see I am footy mad,
I support Bolton Wanderers,
My favourite player is Kevin Davis and Jessi.
Wanderers, Wanderers, Wanderers . . .
I like to watch Bolton with all my mates
And Man Utd is the team I hate!
I play for Bury, Bury North End,
I play in centre mid
And it is all so fab.
I have a bezzie mate who loves a girl.
He's like, 'Abi this,' and, 'Abi that.'
My friend Brad stops playing footy,
To go over to Abi and give her a kiss.
He can't wait until he is 16.

Nathan Young (12)
The Elton High School, Bury

My BFFs

My BFFs are here with me!
Jennie, Abz, Leah, Livi and me!
My BFFs are here with me!
Tell me now why they're here,
My best mates come together,
I'll tell you now, they like me!
My BFFs are now or never,
I love them as they come together!
BFFs till the end!
I'm leaving so I'll be told!
BFFs are never not together!
Best mates till the end,
OMG we're best friends.

Chloe Trippier (12)
The Elton High School, Bury

Football

F eelings are indescribable, scoring a goal for the team you love
and helping them to victory.

O verall the best thing is playing for the team you feel at
home for.

O h my God we just scored a goal, I feel really happy like winning
the lottery.

T otal glory as we lift the cup as a team.

B alls are flying everywhere, we try and control or volley them.

A lways action in the game so we pay attention all the time.

L ook out or heads up we always shout as the ball's in the air.

L earning we do all the time as we make mistakes but we forgive
and we get better.

Findlay Cottam (12)
The Elton High School, Bury

It's My . . .

It's my family
It's my grade
It's my religion
It's my skin colour
It's my hair
It's my weight
It's my make-up
It's my height
They're my friends
They're my clothes
It's my style, not yours
Don't judge me for it.

Dominique Duff (13)
The Elton High School, Bury

Football

F antastic sport, good to play
O ver the moon any day
O val-shaped ball is what you use
T ie tightly your studded football shoes
B last the ball in the net
A mazing feelings in your head
L ots of people chant your name
L ove the feeling, love the game.

Ryan Basnett (12)
The Elton High School, Bury

The Football Life

F un to play.
O n the pitch is green and white.
O n our shirt is 'Walshaw to stay'.
T ie your shoelace very tight.
B uy new shoes every season.
A ll the teams play the game.
L ike your team for every reason.
L ove the game and feel no shame.

Michael Blunt & Harry Moore (11)
The Elton High School, Bury

A Hero's Pride

Bullets speeding through the air,
Empty shells lie everywhere.
Hand me down helmet once worn with pride,
The soldiers armed with nothing to hide.

Fighting for your country,
Fighting with a passion.
While back in the homeland,
They continue to ration.

Adrenaline rushing through his blood,
He enlisted as he thought he should,
But if he knew then as he knows now,
He never would.

The only thing fuelling the battle machine,
The rush of war and the things he's seen.
If he could he would go home,
Or take his family on a trip to Rome.

The supposed hero risks life and limb,
But afterwards who will care for him?
He is a true hero and that is clear,
But would you spare five minutes and a listening ear?

Ryan Taylor (12)
Thornaby Community School, Stockton-on-Tees

140

Our Lives Have Changed

Our lives,
It brought us peace,
Cities linked like bee hives,
Our lives were fitting piece by piece.
Everyone was happy,
Until that day came.

The sun clouded over,
Sirens began to ring,
Were our lives over?
When guns begin to sing,
We went back in time,
It was happening again.

Bombs exploding,
Death came to us,
Houses, lives eroding.
Crushed to the floor.
All he did
Was against us.

Is it possible to rebuild . . .
Death itself?
Our lives,
Not theirs.
They ruined us,
Not even with a warning buzz.

Callum Vernon (13)
Thornaby Community School, Stockton-on-Tees

Uncontrollable

The strange man in the white coat
Couldn't look me in the eyes,
So he sat two seats away,
Unaware I was still the same man.

I stood proud and strong
Knowing things weren't okay,
Leaving my life in hands of a stranger,
Top left of my chest bursting with fear.

All I could think about,
The only thing I could think about,
My family in tears,
My lifelong fears.

My soulmate, my children,
My baby's baby
Growing old without me,
Every day is precious.

So together as one
We must be strong
And all will live
Through the battle of cancer.

Through the battle of cancer,
We'll never give up.

Mary Galloway (12)
Thornaby Community School, Stockton-on-Tees

War Against Time

She is so brave, so strong,
Unaware when her time will arrive,
She has lived so long,
Fighting to survive.

Her time is drawing near,
Life being pulled from her,
Life filled with fear,
A life she can hardly bear.

The years she has lived and lost,
Forgetting her younger years,
Living this long comes with a price,
Like forgetting your hopes and fears.

She fights her age,
She fights herself,
She fights her anger, her rage,
She fights through sickness and through health.

Death is the last one to face
When it's war against time,
Life and death intertwine like a race,
Taking someone, committing no crime.

Adam Parkinson (13)
Thornaby Community School, Stockton-on-Tees

War

All war is about some hate,
Some wars are battles, some are fights,
It leaves the world in a sickly state,
Lasting all those days and nights.

So many people in war have died,
It comes to so many people as a surprise,
It should all be left aside
Because there is no final prize.

Josh Levick (13)
Thornaby Community School, Stockton-on-Tees

143

Over The Top

The artillery began to thunder
Like a rain that never ends.
The ground around me shuddered
As I began to climb.

I was lucky to get over,
Many people, they did fall.
Brothers, comrades, friends and all
Will never go home again.

My heart began to pound
As I ran towards the guns.
Bullets whistled past me
Whilst bombs destroyed the ground.

I was only one of few
Who reached the Germans' trench.
I thought that I was safe,
I thought my work was done.

To this day I still remember
The blood, the death and all.
So many people did fall that day,
Let's never forget them all.

Jessica Fox (13)
Thornaby Community School, Stockton-on-Tees

Why War?

Why war?
It just stops sport
People die more and more

Day turns to dusk
Everywhere there's gun musk
Gas is about
All I can do is shout.

Kye Steven Reaney-Farr (12)
Thornaby Community School, Stockton-on-Tees

144

Cancer Wins The Battle

She lay there still and quiet,
the end had come so quick.
The hard battle was now over,
her heart had had its last tick.

The family sat round waiting
for the tears to start to come.
The deadly silence had been broken,
how her children had no mum.

Cancer had won the battle,
there was nothing left to say.
I could not hold my tears back,
she had left, she was finally taken away.

My mum hugged me tightly
as I cried non-stop tears.
My nana had been taken from me,
now I had to face my fears.

It's hard not being able to see her
and not to have her to care
but she will always be in my heart
and will always be there.

Sophie Clayton (13)
Thornaby Community School, Stockton-on-Tees

Fading Memories

I screamed out in grief,
My tears washing away my blood,
What was I doing there,
Encrusted in gore and mud?
My troops were all gone,
Soon I would be too,
This wasn't a game,
I didn't know what to do.
Dead bodies all around me,
I was the only one still there,
Another bomb went off,
But, truly, no one cared.
The sickening snap
As my leg was finally broken,
I let out a howl of pain
As I was awoken.
Laying safe in my bed,
I sighed in relief,
But I just couldn't let go
Of all the regretful grief.

Charlotte Brown (12)
Thornaby Community School, Stockton-on-Tees

Living The Dream

He wants to join the army to follow his dreams
And sometimes everything's not as it seems
He puts on his kit and begins to walk
When he gets there, there is no time left to talk

In the end he arrives at the war
One bang and his life shuts a door
And he lies there, bullet in the brain
That bullet went through faster than a train
How will they do it, tell his wife and kid?
Everything he'd done, all the good he did.

Stacey Louise Walker (13)
Thornaby Community School, Stockton-on-Tees

146

Waiting

I fell to the ground,
Waiting to be noticed,
I lay there,
Observing my friends fighting for their lives,
But for who?
No one was really at any risk,
Nobody apart from us.

We lay there motionless,
It was deadly quiet,
Aeroplanes flew over us
Like seagulls stalking their prey,
Until the end of the day.

I was one of the fortunate ones,
I made it to the end of the line,
Waiting to be picked up,
Tears rolling down my face,
I felt as if I was in space,
Waiting, waiting for revenge,
I lasted until the very end.

Chloe Gittins (12)
Thornaby Community School, Stockton-on-Tees

A Mother's Grief

Her hands were shaking
As her tears fell,
Her heart was breaking,
She was going through hell.

Her son had now gone,
He was so brave,
But he was hit by a bomb
And now he will journey to the grave.

He went to war,
This gave him a scare,
The thing he saw
Made him care.

You could hear his mother cry,
She started to fret,
She never got to say goodbye
And that is her greatest regret.

Katie Manuel (12)
Thornaby Community School, Stockton-on-Tees

The Way They Went

They know that they are right,
They'll keep going until their last breath,
They'll fight into the night
Until their own death.

The losers will fall down,
We can hear them cry,
Whilst the winners are crowned,
The losers will have died.

In the end the country is mended,
Fear not my friends the war has ended,
All the soldiers gave whatever they could,
They'll go to Heaven, they really should!

Ayesha Saddique (13)
Thornaby Community School, Stockton-on-Tees

 148

Fighting For His Life

Her knees became weak
And her hands began to shake
The most she could do was cry with the pain
She now knew life would never be the same.

Her son had joined the army a while ago
The most he could do she would never know
She'd thought he would have a good life ahead
But not now as he was dead
All she had left of him was a grave
Of course she still knew he was very brave.

As the guns were fired in the evening sky
All she could do was cry and cry
Thinking about her son all day
But in his coffin he did lay.

Chelsea Higgin (13)
Thornaby Community School, Stockton-on-Tees

The Water

As I run down the cold rocks,
Rocks as cold as ice cubes,
My body whooshes from one side to the other,
Splashing left to right.
I run as fast as a cheetah
And I sound like a radio
But a radio with no signal.
The bubbles are floating on top,
Going down with me,
Bubbles the colour of a swan.
Me? I'm clear like a window
And shiny like a diamond.
I'm still running,
Running as fast as I've ever run before,
I'm not going to stop
Until I reach the bottom of the fall.

Katie Owen (12)
Ysgol Dyffryn Nantlle, Penygroes

149

Goodbye

How can you let them go?
Seeing the sad children's faces
Just passing you by
How can you live without them?

Knowing it is the right thing
But still regretting it
Seeing the children cry
How will you go on?

Will you ever see them again?
To see the children smiling
Knowing you will do anything
To see the smile.

There they go
Off on their own
Did you kiss them on their cheek?
And would you like to hug them one more time?

They're waving goodbye
What do you do?
Is the war ever going to end?
Am I going to be OK?

Now they go
See the train leave
Children waving goodbye
Mothers waving back
Bye bye my dear one.

Elin Llwyd Williams (12)
Ysgol Dyffryn Nantlle, Penygroes

The Monkey

Me, a monkey,
Nearly every person's dream,
I am just free,
I feel so alive and energised.

Some people describe me
As the giant nit,
Why? Because I am big,
I am brown
And moving around.

We all swing from tree to tree,
I tell you we are free, free,
It is so fun and cool,
You can't resist having a try at home
Because you have the time of your life.

I am hairy and cute,
I am furry and fuzzy,
Maybe I might be funky
And maybe a little chunky
But remember I am a monkey.

Caitlin Tocker (12)
Ysgol Dyffryn Nantlle, Penygroes

The Fearsome Tiger

As I lie here every nightfall, every daybreak
Watching the people pass
Going back and forth
And looking in amazement at my family.

As I walk back and forth
I hold in my never-ending anger
I have no patience left
I am forever waiting for my revenge.

Stripping every piece of meat off my enemies
And throwing the carcass aside
Everything that comes in here dies.

They destroyed my home
And nearly me with it
I roar and growl every day, every nightfall
In anger, my never-ending anger
And wait . . .
For revenge.

Oscar William Trower (12)
Ysgol Dyffryn Nantlle, Penygroes

The Giraffe

You have a long neck my friend,
I never thought it would end.
When you ate from the tree
So elegantly and free,
I thought to myself,
What are you doing here my friend?

I saw you standing by the fence,
All alone and sad,
I felt the urge to cuddle you,
I only wish I had.
But I could not let go
Of the hand that held me so . . . tight.

Helen Davies (11)
Ysgol Dyffryn Nantlle, Penygroes

Spider

Look at me,
I make children cry.
I don't even try,
My face just makes children cry.

I like to walk up the wall,
But sometimes I just fall.
Oh boy! Oh boy!
It's just too hard.

I have lost my best friends,
They were all about the trends
But not me,
No, not me.

Whatever, whatever,
I thought I would live forever.
But now there are people,
Well think again,
No one lives forever.

Shân Elin Jones (12)
Ysgol Dyffryn Nantlle, Penygroes

Zoo

The monkeys in the cage,
They stand and stare so strange.
The people pass and wave as they leave

The lions pounce and roar
As they roam around the floor,
Going nowhere but round in circles
They pass and slowly collapse in a ball.

The giraffes are all so tall
Looking out at us all.
They think it is silly that we look
Them up when they can all see over the wall.

Patrick Noone (12)
Ysgol Dyffryn Nantlle, Penygroes

The River

Cold runny water
Rushing down the river,
Cold as ice,
Blue like the sky.

Skeleton trees hug the bank
Casting shadows on the shiny water,
The massive sound creating an icy feeling,
Ghostly shadows on the icy cold water.

Gushing water creating a huge sound
That echoes through the valley,
Misty vapour hangs upon the pool
As the water runs towards the sea.

Emyr Fon Parry (11)
Ysgol Dyffryn Nantlle, Penygroes

A Poem Fe Me Is . . .

A poem fe me is . . .
De riddim,
De beat,
It makes me wanna move me feet.

A poem fe me is . . .
Expressing me feelings
And me emotion,
It makes me have motion.

A poem fe me is . . .
A flowing sentence
Like a wave on a beach
Which is as smooth as a peach.

A poem fe me is . . .
De meaning of each word
Making sense,
Nothing can be tense.

Ffion Williams (13)
Ysgol Eifionydd, Porthmadog

154

Song And Glory

Dis li'l poem makes de birds sing wid joy,
Make da father stop hittin' da boy.
Dis li'l poem 'ere sends riddum tru your bones,
No sadness, no depression, no boring long drones.
So let da pretty birds tell a story
'Bout song, 'bout glory.

Be no difficult words or rhyme,
Nor any stories 'bout blood an' crime.
Tink more happy, sweet songs of love
And of heroes who were sent from above.

Der is no doubt some tears will drop,
'Bout no doom, no gloom, just happy days to come,
'Bout sunshine and rain, great for some.

Now clap your hands to de beat,
Dis ain't no ordinary feat.
'Bout a man who saved a lot of lives
An' deserves a billion high fives.

Travelled thru rivers, over mountains,
He got wet and got grass stains.
All dis to save some unknown souls,
Dis man has saved many skulls.

How was dis achieved?
Simple, no drugs, no weed.
Just a sense of beat and a li'l somethin' to eat,
Could make any bird tweet, tweet, tweet.

Dis li'l poem makes da birds sing wid joy,
Make da father stop hittin' da boy.
Dis li'l poem 'ere sends riddum tru your bones,
No sadness, no depression, no boring long drones.
So let da pretty birds tell a story,
'Bout song, 'bout glory.

Steffan Daniel Lane (14)
Ysgol Eifionydd, Porthmadog

155

Footsteps Echo Poetry

Down 'ere we don't give a damn,
Not 'bout what society say,
Not 'bout what that ol' man fink.

Dese words what don' mean nuffink,
De Primo,
De cabinet,
De law.

We jus' tryin' to get on.

An' when it comes to jail,
No difference, in or out.

Dere's much pain.

No relief.

We do what we want,
An' we shout about it.

Dere's always been poetry,
Always on paper,
On the wall,
In graffiti,
Tattoo on our heart.

Now we don't quake,
We've no' afraid,
Not o' running blues,
Nor ov avin' no cash,
We not 'fraid.

Not o' knives nor needles.

Our blood run free
An' we don't weep.

Our poetry ain't written, nor sunny,
Our poetry ain' never been heard,
But our poetry echo deep down,
Moving with our heavy heartbeat.

We all held prisoner,
We wanna make some noise.

So we'll rattle our chains.

Baden Vaughan Roberts (14)
Ysgol Eifionydd, Porthmadog

Da Poem For Bob Marley

Dis poem's like waterfalls' drops,
De waves come crashin' wivout no stops.
Dis poetry is like made fe jammin',
Free li'l birds on me doorstep singin'.
Da buffalo soulja from Africa
Will come down 'n' smoke a bit o' ganja.
Let's get da party started,
We'll dance for hours unguarded.
It's like da breeze from Jamaica
Blowin' freely full a pleasa,
Giv' me tinglin' in me toes,
In me soul it blows.
Dis poem's like propa,
Hear da steel drums go bonga,
Drummin' in Africa,
Right thru to Jamaica
'N' down to da bottom of America.
Dis poem is da fire burnin' in me heart
'N' when I pop down to de Wall-e-Mart
I remember 'n' cherish da fact I'm alive,
Dat's why my generation
Stand togeva 'n' strive!
Wiv Marley's sweet melodies
We dance and we jive!

Cedron Sion (14)
Ysgol Eifionydd, Porthmadog

Untitled

When de tears fall after hearin' dat one word,
Death.
When de love gets too strong, you have to take a
Breath,
Is it true?
When de riddum reminds you of that special person
Den de beat tru your feet
And de happiness is complete.

But sometimes de mood changes de scene,
De door has shut, you want to
Scream.
De good times only happen in movies,
Den reality is dreamin' wid de sweet taste in your mouth,
Chocolate.

Ye have de poems where dey talk about rubbish,
Yet dat last word might make de mind tink,
De poet was writin' der emotions
As they were feelin' de devotion.
You can't judge a poem unless ye know de meanin'
Den it comes to an endin'
When we walk up de mountain.
But den ye realise, it been a dream,
So you're on de mountain, den dat one step,
Dat one step
Makes a fraction of my
Love
Fill the air
And I fall in love wid you
All over again.

Megan Williams (14)
Ysgol Eifionydd, Porthmadog

15 8

African Flower

Dis poem is lyk a flower,
It cools me down,
It takes out all de tension.
Dis flower brings out me emotion,
It gyvs me lyf, it tyke me to a different world,
It's more lyk me illusion.
Its scent so strong, yet delusional,
Its world so beautiful, so dimensional.
I'm a chick with strong yet simple taste,
Mess with me an' you'll be gone in flames.
Love me an' you'll feel me embrace,
Dis flower brings out me grace,
Hidden, an' out of dis place.
Dis flower is lyk me spaceship, me ride to outer space,
Dis flower is me African beat,
A place for me to dream,
Me ultimate place of retreat.

It blooms in summer, autumn, winter and spring,
Its glow so wild an' loud, lyk me expensive bling.
I smell it, I love it,
I can't live without it.
You kill it,
You kill me.
It lives deep within me,
My lyf,
Ma swagga.
It describes me betta,
Ma African beat
Lingers in me forever.

Temalangeni Dlamini (15)
Ysgol Eifionydd, Porthmadog

Dis Poetry

Poetry is lyf,
Poetry is cool,
Yu can make it anything,
Just don't be a fool.
Poetry yu can sing,
Poetry yu can rap,
Writing a poem is easy,
Yu can make people laugh.

I've tried to learn Shakespeare
But it's blydi fatiguing,
I prefer dis kind of poem
Cos dis is wat I believe in,
In dis poetry,
There ain't no big vocabulary
Cos I want yu all to understand meh.
When u read dis poem
Ur hips start to move.
Clap ur hands,
Feel the groove.
Now it's tym to say goodbye
Remember dis meaning
Until you die!

Alaw Medi Jones (14)
Ysgol Eifionydd, Porthmadog

16o

Freedom

Freedom is . . .
Livin' me life,
Bein' myself,
Ignorin' de rules,
Expressin' me feelin's,
Not worrying about life's meanin'.

Freedom is . . .
Being wild,
Havin' fun,
Takin' risks,
Expressin' me feelin's,
Not worrying about life's meanin'.

Freedom is . . .
Lovin' ya life,
Believin' in ya self,
Being happy,
Expressin' me feelin's,
Not worrying about life's meanin'.

Etta Morgan Trumper (14)
Ysgol Eifionydd, Porthmadog

Dis Is Poetry

Dis is a poem.
Poetry is what surrounds you,
What you see every day.
Poetry is life written on paper,
Den spoken in riddum and rime.

Poetry is feelin's and believe ins,
Happiness, sadness and lyf,
Day to day happenin's
An' everythin' above.

Poetry can be any size,
Long or short, or one or two lines,
But in me case I don't have time,
So it depends if I get to de end of de line.

I've nearly come to de end of me time,
So I'll finish off wid a bit of a rime,
Just to shortly say goodbye,
Remember a poem is spoken wid de eye.

Erin Hàf O'Donnell (13)
Ysgol Eifionydd, Porthmadog

Poetry Is

Dis poetry is like de big bird
It fly so high
It go thru de wind
And over dem houses

You can look and paint
But it'll never go
Only in de night
Also it create a shadow
It make different patterns
It could make rain
But not on a sunny day
That would be a shame.

Llinos Mared Evans (13)
Ysgol Eifionydd, Porthmadog

162

Poetry Is . . .

Poetry is de most awesome ting in de world,
It makes ye feel happy,
It makes ye feel sad,
It hit ye heart,
It designed fe listenin' an' fe learnin',
Poetry keep ye apart from de world,
But don't worry dey know ye dere,
It help ye sleep,
It keep ye alive,
It's de most awesome ting in de world.

Daniel Griffiths (13)
Ysgol Eifionydd, Porthmadog

Dis Is Poetry

Dis is poetry,
It's what you see thru your eyes,
Poetry is life written in words,
Expressions never die.

Dis is poetry,
Feelings, touching,
Surroundings all around,
Dis rhyme will never bring you down.

Dis is poetry,
Finish with one more rhyme,
Never speak with your mouth,
Think with the feelings all around.

Catrin Richards (14)
Ysgol Eifionydd, Porthmadog

The Aliens Are Coming!
(Based on 'The Aliens Have Landed' by Kenn Nesbitt)

The aliens have landed!
It's scary, but they're here.
They landed their flying saucers
Through our atmosphere.
Out they climbed towards our school
And up they sat upon a stool
As we all know that aliens are cruel.

Their hands are greasy tentacles.
Their heads are weird machines.
Their bodies look like cauliflower
And smell like dead sardines.
They wear these ties,
They wear these skirts.
There is a bell so we alert
That the aliens are coming.

And if you want to see these
Bossy, unattractive creatures,
You'll find them working in your school;
They've all got jobs as teachers!

Alex Starr (12)
Ysgol John Bright, Llandudno

Don't Be Judged

She, like a book,
Judged by the cover
Or still unread?
Some read half,
Some just the end,
If you want to know her
You have to read
All of her.
No skipping chapters,
Everything!

Dion Brisque (15)
Ysgol John Bright, Llandudno

Danny Boy

I know a lovely horse, which is big and bay,
He loves to munch on his delicious hay.

His name is Danny
And he's ever so happy.

He canters and gallops through the green, green grass,
You don't even see him pass!

He moves so elegantly through the air
With his lovely bay long hair.

When I ride him I feel so cool,
Moving quick and feeling so tall!

When he jumps over a jump he feels so high,
He feels he's going to go off and fly!

When he rears, when he bucks,
He's so scary to touch!

He comes from the Yorkshire Dales
And loves to munch, like I said, on his bales!

He will always have a special place in my heart
And we will never be apart!

We are best friends!

Helena Gull (13)
Ysgol John Bright, Llandudno

My Sweet Fudge
(In loving memory of Fudge, 25th December 2006 - 14th April 2010, aged 3)

Fudge was a furry hamster
Who loved to be top jamster.
When she used to play in her ball,
She used to play until she would fall.
She had big black eyes
Like tiny little flies.
She loved to run, she loved to play,
She loved to have fun all day.
She even had a friend to play with,
Which was . . . the fridge!
Then she died and went all cold,
Although she was getting quite old.
I loved her so,
I'm glad I know
That although she was so small,
Her memory shall remain in the hearts of all.

Rachel Wilson (12)
Ysgol John Bright, Llandudno

Young Writers Information

We hope you have enjoyed reading this book - and that you will continue to enjoy it in the coming years.

If you like reading and writing poetry drop us a line, or give us a call, and we'll send you a free information pack.

Alternatively if you would like to order further copies of this book or any of our other titles, then please give us a call or log onto our website at www.youngwriters.co.uk.

Young Writers Information
Remus House
Coltsfoot Drive
Peterborough
PE2 9JX
(01733) 890066